# FUN 學美國英語 閱讀寫作 課本

# AMERICAN SCHOOL TEXTBOOK

GRADE 5

MP3 🔊

## Reading & Writing

作者 Christine Dugan / Leslie Huber / Margot Kinberg / Miriam Meyers　譯者 林育珊

# FUN 學美國英語 閱讀寫作課本 5
## American School Textbook: Reading & Writing

| | |
|---|---|
| 作　　者 | Christine Dugan / Leslie Huber / Margot Kinberg / Miriam Meyers |
| 審　　定 | Judy Majewski |
| 譯　　者 | 林育珊 |
| 編　　輯 | 呂紹柔 |

| | |
|---|---|
| 封面設計 | 郭瀞暄 |
| 內文排版 | 田慧盈／郭瀞暄 |
| 製程管理 | 宋建文 |
| 出 版 者 | 寂天文化事業股份有限公司 |
| 電　　話 | +886-(0)2-2365-9739 |
| 傳　　真 | +886-(0)2-2365-9835 |
| 網　　址 | www.icosmos.com.tw |
| 讀者服務 | onlineservice@icosmos.com.tw |
| 出版日期 | 2013 年 10 月 初版一刷　(080101) |

郵撥帳號　1998620-0　　寂天文化事業股份有限公司

· 劃撥金額 600（含）元以上者，郵資免費。

· 訂購金額 600 元以下者，加收 65 元運費。

【若有破損，請寄回更換，謝謝。】

# HOW TO USE THIS BOOK

The **Skill Overview** provides background information about the skill focus for the lesson.

**Reading Passage**

The **Lesson Number** and **Reading Skill** are clearly identified.

The **Reading Tip** provides guidance for reading each lesson.

Critical **Vocabulary** words from the passage are listed.

**Power Up** summarizes the key terminology and ideas for each lesson.

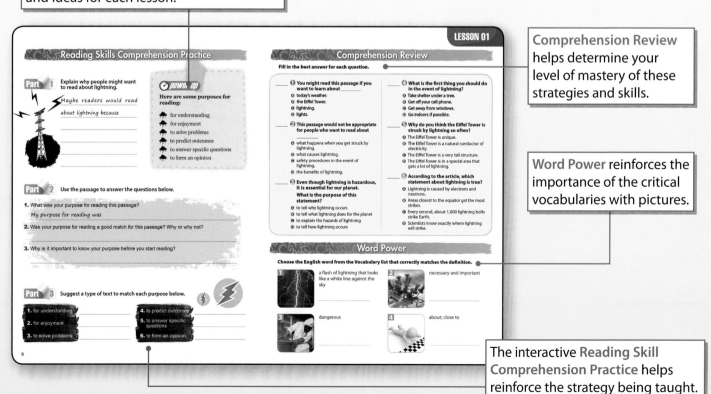

**Comprehension Review** helps determine your level of mastery of these strategies and skills.

**Word Power** reinforces the importance of the critical vocabularies with pictures.

The interactive **Reading Skill Comprehension Practice** helps reinforce the strategy being taught.

# **C**ontents **C**hart

| Reading Skill | Subject |
| --- | --- |
| Purpose for Reading | Science |
| Previewing | Social Studies ★ History and Geography |
| Conflict and Resolution | Language and Literature |
| Making Inferences | Social Studies ★ History and Geography |
| Main Idea and Details | Language and Literature |
| Titles to Predict | Social Studies ★ History and Geography |
| Selecting Reading Material | Language and Literature |
| Character Development | Language and Literature |
| Logical Order | Social Studies ★ History and Geography |
| Headings to Determine Main Ideas | Language and Literature |
| Topic Sentences to Predict | Science |
| Literary Devices | Language and Literature |
| Cause and Effect | Social Studies ★ History and Geography |
| Paraphrasing | Science |
| Typeface | Social Studies ★ History and Geography |
| Reflecting on What Has Been Learned | Social Studies ★ History and Geography |
| Use of Language | Language and Literature |
| Compare and Contrast | Science |
| Adjust and Extend Knowledge | Science |
| Topic Sentences to Determine Main Ideas | Social Studies ★ History and Geography |
| Author's Devices | Language and Literature |
| Author's Point of View | Language and Literature |
| Drawing Conclusions | Science |
| Proposition and Support | Social Studies ★ History and Geography |
| Graphic Features | Mathematics |
| Monitoring Reading Strategies | Science |
| Captions to Determine Main Ideas | Social Studies ★ History and Geography |
| Chronological Order | Social Studies ★ History and Geography |
| Fact and Opinion | Visual Arts |
| Questioning | Social Studies ★ History and Geography |

# LOOK OUT FOR LIGHTNING

## Skill Overview

All meaningful reading needs a purpose. When readers understand the purpose for reading a particular text, they can select the appropriate reading strategies to meet their reading goals.

**Lightning bolts streak through the sky toward the ground.**

🎧 01

Lightning, one of nature's most powerful forces, can kill people and animals, **destroy** buildings and trees, and start raging forest fires. Although lightning usually comes with a thunderstorm, it can also occur during snowstorms, during sandstorms, and in the clouds of a volcanic eruption. Every second, **approximately** 100 lightning **bolts strike** Earth. Areas closest to the equator get the most strikes.

Lightning maintains the electrical balance in clouds. Everything has tiny **particles** called *electrons* and *protons*. Lightning occurs when electrons move toward protons. Electrons jump at high speeds to protons within the same cloud, in another cloud, or on the ground. When electrons move, the air gets so hot that its temperature exceeds that of the Sun's surface. The air glows, and the burst of extreme heat makes the moist air explode, causing the sound waves we call *thunder*. That's why a clap of thunder always follows a lightning flash.

You have probably seen jagged lightning bolts streaking from the sky toward the ground. Usually these bolts hit the tallest thing in the area. In fact, the Eiffel Tower in Paris gets struck by lightning dozens of times each year. The people who design skyscrapers know this; therefore, skyscrapers have systems to keep lightning strikes from causing damage.

No one knows exactly when or where lightning will strike, but you can take steps to avoid getting hit by it. If you can, go inside at the first sign of lightning—it's much safer indoors. However, lightning can still reach into a building, so don't talk on the phone or stand at a window. Do not swim if there is lightning in the area. If you are out in a boat, get down inside the cabin. If you are caught outside away from buildings, get into a car or a truck. Never take shelter under a tree, as trees can be struck by lightning, and the electricity can transfer through them and into you.

Even though lightning is **hazardous**, it is **essential** for our planet. Every bolt produces **ozone** gas, which protects us from the Sun's strong radiation. Each lightning bolt also cleans the air by making pieces of pollution fall to the ground.

## Vocabulary

**destroy**
to damage something so badly that it cannot be used

**approximately**
about; close to

**bolt**
a flash of lightning that looks like a white line against the sky

**strike**
to hit with force

**particle**
an extremely small piece of matter

**hazardous**
dangerous

**essential**
necessary and important

**ozone**
a poisonous form of oxygen

**The Eiffel Tower in Paris gets struck by lightning dozens of times each year.**

HISTORIC NWS COLLECTION

5

# Reading Skills Comprehension Practice

**Part 1** Explain why people might want to read about lightning.

Maybe readers would read

about lightning because

_____

_____

_____

_____

**Part 2** Use the passage to answer the questions below.

**1.** What was your purpose for reading this passage?

My purpose for reading was

_____

**2.** Was your purpose for reading a good match for this passage? Why or why not?

_____

**3.** Why is it important to know your purpose before you start reading?

_____

**Part 3** Suggest a type of text to match each purpose below.

**1.** for understanding _____

**2.** for enjoyment _____

**3.** to solve problems _____

**4.** to predict outcomes _____

**5.** to answer specific questions _____

**6.** to form an opinion _____

# Comprehension Review

**Fill in the best answer for each question.**

_____ ❶ **You might read this passage if you want to learn about _____**
- Ⓐ today's weather.
- Ⓑ the Eiffel Tower.
- Ⓒ lightning.
- Ⓓ lights.

_____ ❷ **This passage would not be appropriate for people who want to read about _____**
- Ⓐ what happens when you get struck by lightning.
- Ⓑ what causes lightning.
- Ⓒ safety procedures in the event of lightning.
- Ⓓ the benefits of lightning.

_____ ❸ **_Even though lightning is hazardous, it is essential for our planet._ What is the purpose of this statement?**
- Ⓐ to tell why lightning occurs
- Ⓑ to tell what lightning does for the planet
- Ⓒ to explain the hazards of lightning
- Ⓓ to tell how lightning occurs

_____ ❹ **What is the first thing you should do in the event of lightning?**
- Ⓐ Take shelter under a tree.
- Ⓑ Get off your cell phone.
- Ⓒ Get away from windows.
- Ⓓ Go indoors if possible.

_____ ❺ **Why do you think the Eiffel Tower is struck by lightning so often?**
- Ⓐ The Eiffel Tower is unique.
- Ⓑ The Eiffel Tower is a natural conductor of electricity.
- Ⓒ The Eiffel Tower is a very tall structure.
- Ⓓ The Eiffel Tower is in a special area that gets a lot of lightning.

_____ ❻ **According to the article, which statement about lightning is true?**
- Ⓐ Lightning is caused by electrons and neutrons.
- Ⓑ Areas closest to the equator get the most strikes.
- Ⓒ Every second, about 1,000 lightning bolts strike Earth.
- Ⓓ Scientists know exactly where lightning will strike.

# Word Power

**Choose the English word from the Vocabulary list that correctly matches the definition.**

1. a flash of lightning that looks like a white line against the sky

_____

2. necessary and important

_____

3. dangerous

_____

4. about; close to

_____

# The Death of a President

**A reward poster for Booth and his accomplices**

SURRAT.     BOOTH.     HAROLD.

War Department, Washington, April 20, 1865,

👉 $100,000 REWARD!

# THE MURDERER

Of our late beloved President, Abraham Lincoln,

## IS STILL AT LARGE.

# $50,000 REWARD

Will be paid by this Department for his apprehension, in addition to any reward offered by Municipal Authorities or State Executives.

# $25,000 REWARD

Will be paid for the apprehension of JOHN H. SURRATT, one of Booth's Accomplices.

# $25,000 REWARD

Will be paid for the apprehension of David C. Harold, another of Booth's accomplices.

LIBERAL REWARDS will be paid for any information that shall conduce to the arrest of either of the above-named criminals, or their accomplices.

All persons harboring or secreting the said persons, or either of them, or aiding or assisting their concealment or escape, will be treated as accomplices in the murder of the President and the attempted assassination of the Secretary of State, and shall be subject to trial before a Military Commission and the punishment of DEATH.

Let the stain of innocent blood be removed from the land by the arrest and punishment of the murderers.

All good citizens are exhorted to aid public justice on this occasion. Every man should consider his own conscience charged with this solemn duty, and rest neither night nor day until it be accomplished.

### EDWIN M. STANTON, Secretary of War.

DESCRIPTIONS.—BOOTH is Five Feet 7 or 8 inches high, slender build, high forehead, black hair, black eyes, and wears a heavy black moustache.

JOHN H. SURRAT is about 5 feet, 9 inches. Hair rather thin and dark; eyes rather light; no beard. Would weigh 145 or 150 pounds. Complexion rather pale and clear, with color in his cheeks. Wore light clothes of fine quality. Shoulders square; cheek bones rather prominent; chin narrow; ears projecting at the top; forehead rather low and square, but broad. Parts his hair on the right side; neck rather long. His lips are firmly set. A slim man.

DAVID C. HAROLD is five feet six inches high, hair dark, eyes dark, eyebrows rather heavy, full face, nose short, hand short and fleshy, feet small, instep high, round bodied, naturally quick and active, slightly closes his eyes when looking at a person.

NOTICE.—In addition to the above, State and other authorities have offered rewards amounting to almost one hundred thousand dollars, making an aggregate of about TWO HUNDRED THOUSAND DOLLARS.

**John Wilkes Booth**

**President Lincoln**

cc by Adam Cuerden

## Skill Overview

**Previewing** the title, headings, pictures, and textual clues before reading can help readers **identify the important concepts** in a text. Previewing also allows readers to **activate prior knowledge**, **develop an interest in the text**, and **formulate questions and predictions** about it.

The U.S. Civil War ended on April 9, 1865, when Confederate General Robert E. Lee **surrendered** to Union General Ulysses S. Grant. The two men met and signed an **agreement** to end the war.

Most Southerners were upset that the South had lost the war. John Wilkes Booth was among them. Booth wanted to be a hero to the South. So he and some others created a plan to kill President Abraham Lincoln.

On April 14, 1865, Lincoln **attended** a play at Ford's Theatre in Washington, D.C. He was sitting with his wife and other guests in a special **balcony**. Booth **approached** the balcony where Lincoln was sitting. Lincoln's guard had left his post, so no one stopped Booth as he shot Lincoln in the head. Booth then boldly jumped from the balcony onto the stage. As he escaped the theater, Booth shouted, "Sic semper tyrannis!" which is Latin for "thus always to **tyrants**." He meant that all tyrants, which is how he viewed Lincoln, should be killed. Booth used a horse to **escape** from Ford's Theatre and ride to Virginia.

Sadly, Lincoln died the next day. His vice president, Andrew Johnson, became the seventeenth president of the United States.

Booth thought that people in the South would be proud of what he had done, but this was not the case. Most Southerners were upset over Lincoln's death because Lincoln would have wanted a peaceful Reconstruction. Now, they would be forced to deal with Congress instead of Lincoln, and they were not sure what demands the congressmen would make.

Federal troops found Booth hiding in a barn in Virginia. He refused to give up, so the troops took action by setting the barn on fire. Eventually, troopers shot into the barn, killing Booth. Later, the other people involved in the **assassination** plan were hanged.

# Reading Skills Comprehension Practice

 As readers preview a text, they should remember that authors often purposefully provide clues that hint at what is to come. This technique is called **foreshadowing**.

**Part 1** Fill in the first column of the chart below with your predictions about the passage based on the title and pictures. Then finish the second column after you listen to and read the passage.

| Predictions | Confirmed by the Text? | Explanation |
|---|---|---|
| **1.** *Booth killed Lincoln.* | YES   NO | **1.** *Booth shot Lincoln.* |
| **2.** | YES   NO | **2.** |
| **3.** | YES   NO | **3.** |
| **4.** | YES   NO | **4.** |

**Part 2** List the words or phrases that are foreshadowing clues.

**1.** *wanted to be a hero to the South*

**2.**

**3.**

**4.**

10

# Comprehension Review

**Fill in the best answer for each question.**

_____ **❶ The title is a good clue that this passage will be about _____**
- Ⓐ what happened when a president died.
- Ⓑ how presidents are elected.
- Ⓒ where the president lives.
- Ⓓ who can be president.

_____ **❷ What kind of passage is this?**
- Ⓐ a list of instructions
- Ⓑ a poem
- Ⓒ a story about an event
- Ⓓ a letter

_____ **❸ The first sentence tells you that this event happened _____**
- Ⓐ during the American Revolutionary War.
- Ⓑ when the U.S. Civil War ended.
- Ⓒ last week.
- Ⓓ during World War II.

_____ **❹ The people who helped Booth plan the assassination were probably _____**
- Ⓐ never caught.
- Ⓑ members of Lincoln's family.
- Ⓒ from the North.
- Ⓓ from the South.

_____ **❺ Why did Booth kill President Lincoln?**
- Ⓐ He wanted to be president.
- Ⓑ He wanted to be a hero to the South.
- Ⓒ He was upset that the South won the war.
- Ⓓ He was upset that Lincoln went to Ford's Theater.

_____ **❻ The Civil War ended _____**
- Ⓐ on April 9, 1865.
- Ⓑ at Ford's Theater.
- Ⓒ when Lincoln was killed.
- Ⓓ when Booth died.

# Word Power

**Choose the English word from the Vocabulary list that correctly matches the definition.**

 the upstairs seats in a theater

_____

 the killing of an important person

_____

 to get free from something

_____

 to give up completely

_____

# GREEN THUMBS

## Skill Overview

The plot of a story may include a problem, or conflict, and a solution, or resolution. The conflict, often identified at the beginning of a story, is a key part of the plot or action of the story. The writer usually puts the resolution at the end.

 03

I griped and moaned the entire day because my parents were making me work on the neighborhood project. It was just the ugly, old vacant lot around the corner. It was overflowing with **weeds**, greasy fast-food wrappers, old newspapers, broken glass, and every other kind of disgusting trash you can imagine. As I **contemplated** the scene that morning, I thought, "I bet there are snakes in there, too." I would rather have been anywhere else.

There were 20 of us—a variety of ages and sizes—ready to work that day. The idea that this awful mess could be cleaned, let alone made into a garden showplace, seemed unlikely. I **suspect** we were all **wondering** where to begin when Mr. Hernandez finally said, "The only way to do it is to just start." Then he divided the lot into fourths with string and assigned five people to each **quadrant**.

By lunchtime, I was hot, sweaty, and grimy, but also grateful that my dad had made me wear gloves. The rusty cans and shards of glass were terrible! But we had filled 50 trash bags with garbage and were ready to pull weeds. Now it was time to get a noseful of pollen and go into an allergic sneeze-fest, itching and scratching all the way.

At day's end, I had to admit that the lot looked better—bare, but better. My dad started to rototill the dirt. A **rototiller** is a kind of personal-size tractor that you manage like a lawn mower. It has a gas motor, which drives the rotating blades and pushes it along, and blades that lift and turn the dirt in preparation for planting. Watching Dad's shoulders strain and his arms jostle, I thought how he and the rototiller were a team—like a farmer driving his mechanical earth-eating mule.

Although that first day was the toughest, in the weekends that followed, we made rows in the dirt, planted flower and vegetable seeds, **fertilized**, watered, and weeded. After about two weeks, I stopped griping. The plants had started popping up—first the lettuce, then the beans and squash. They grew so fast, I couldn't believe it. Some days, a bean plant would grow an inch!

Now, two months later, I like to go there to see what new flowers are ready to pop and to talk to people and enjoy the sights. Tonight it suddenly hit me what a good thing we did. I realized how proud I am to have participated. The vegetables will go to the food pantry, and I'm **responsible** for picking bouquets for the nursing home. An eyesore that people avoided has become a pretty patch of green—a place that everyone can enjoy.

## Vocabulary

**weed**
any wild plant that grows in an unwanted place

**contemplate**
to think about something carefully

**suspect**
to think or believe something is true or probable

**wonder**
to ask yourself questions

✪**quadrant**
one of four parts

✪**rototiller**
a personal-size tractor with rotating blades that lift and turn dirt in preparation for planting

**fertilize**
to spread a natural or chemical substance on land or plants to improve growth

**responsible**
having the duty of taking care of someone or something

# Reading Skills Comprehension Practice

 **Part 1** Describe the conflict in this story. Then guess how the author will resolve the conflict.

*The conflict in the story is . . .; I think the author will . . .*

_____

_____

_____

**Part 2** Answer the questions below based on the passage.

**1. What is the resolution of this conflict?**

_____

_____

_____

**2. How is this resolution similar to or different from your prediction in Part 1?**

_____

_____

_____

**Part 3** Write a short story below. Include both a conflict and a resolution in your story.

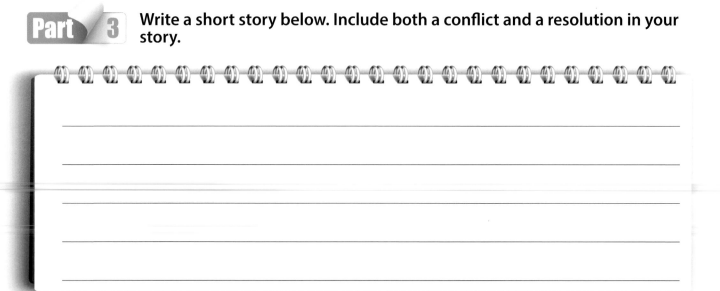

# Comprehension Review

**Fill in the best answer for each question.**

_____ ❶ **The conflict in the story is between** _____

 Ⓐ the narrator and Mr. Hernandez.
 Ⓑ the narrator's parents and some neighbors.
 Ⓒ the narrator and some neighbors.
 Ⓓ the narrator and his parents.

_____ ❷ **Why does the narrator gripe about his parents?**

 Ⓐ They don't like the neighborhood project.
 Ⓑ They are planting a garden.
 Ⓒ They are making him work on the neighborhood project.
 Ⓓ They are using the rototiller.

_____ ❸ **What stops the narrator's griping and ends the conflict?**

 Ⓐ seeing the plants grow
 Ⓑ talking to his parents
 Ⓒ using the rototiller
 Ⓓ visiting a neighbor

_____ ❹ **What is a rototiller used for?**

 Ⓐ getting rid of garbage
 Ⓑ planting seeds
 Ⓒ chopping up leaves
 Ⓓ preparing soil for planting

_____ ❺ **Who is likely in charge of the neighborhood project?**

 Ⓐ the narrator
 Ⓑ Mr. Hernandez
 Ⓒ the narrator's father
 Ⓓ the narrator's brother

_____ ❻ **What caused the narrator's allergy attack?**

 Ⓐ the rototiller
 Ⓑ the trash
 Ⓒ the weeds
 Ⓓ the vegetables

# Word Power

**Choose the English word from the Vocabulary list that correctly matches the definition.**

 one of four parts

_____

 a personal-size tractor with rotating blades that lift and turn dirt in preparation for planting

_____

 to think or believe something is true or probable

_____

 to think about something carefully

_____

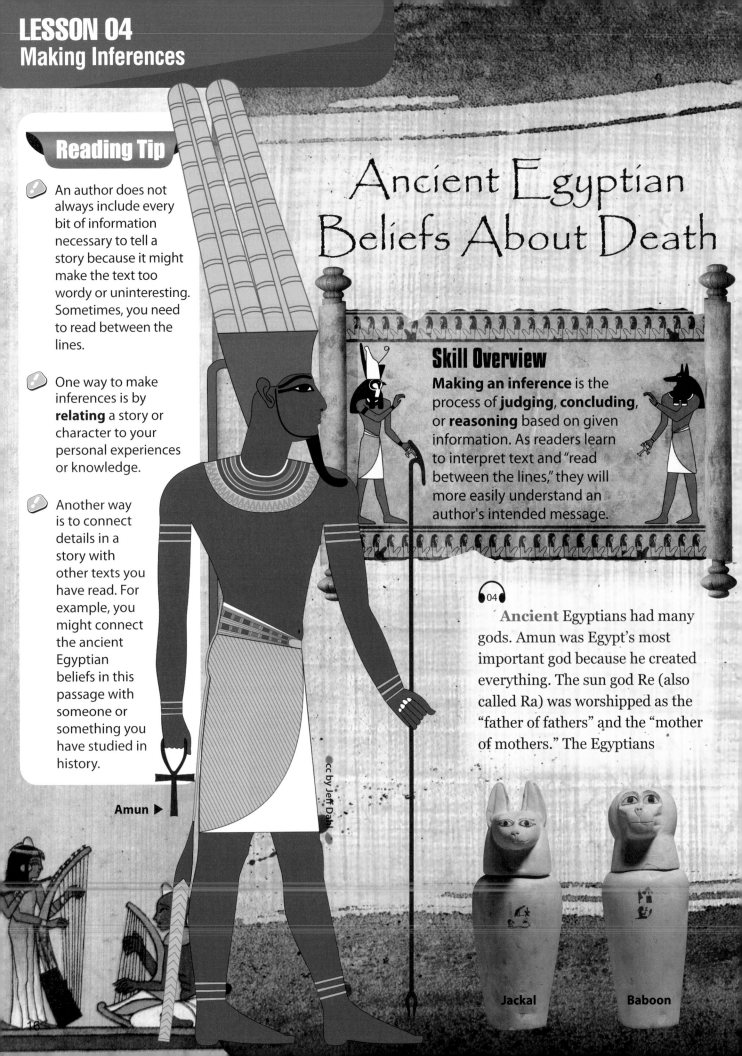

## Reading Tip

An author does not always include every bit of information necessary to tell a story because it might make the text too wordy or uninteresting. Sometimes, you need to read between the lines.

One way to make inferences is by **relating** a story or character to your personal experiences or knowledge.

Another way is to connect details in a story with other texts you have read. For example, you might connect the ancient Egyptian beliefs in this passage with someone or something you have studied in history.

**Amun ▶**

# Ancient Egyptian Beliefs About Death

## Skill Overview

**Making an inference** is the process of **judging**, **concluding**, or **reasoning** based on given information. As readers learn to interpret text and "read between the lines," they will more easily understand an author's intended message.

🎧 04

**Ancient** Egyptians had many gods. Amun was Egypt's most important god because he created everything. The sun god Re (also called Ra) was worshipped as the "father of fathers" and the "mother of mothers." The Egyptians

**Jackal**

**Baboon**

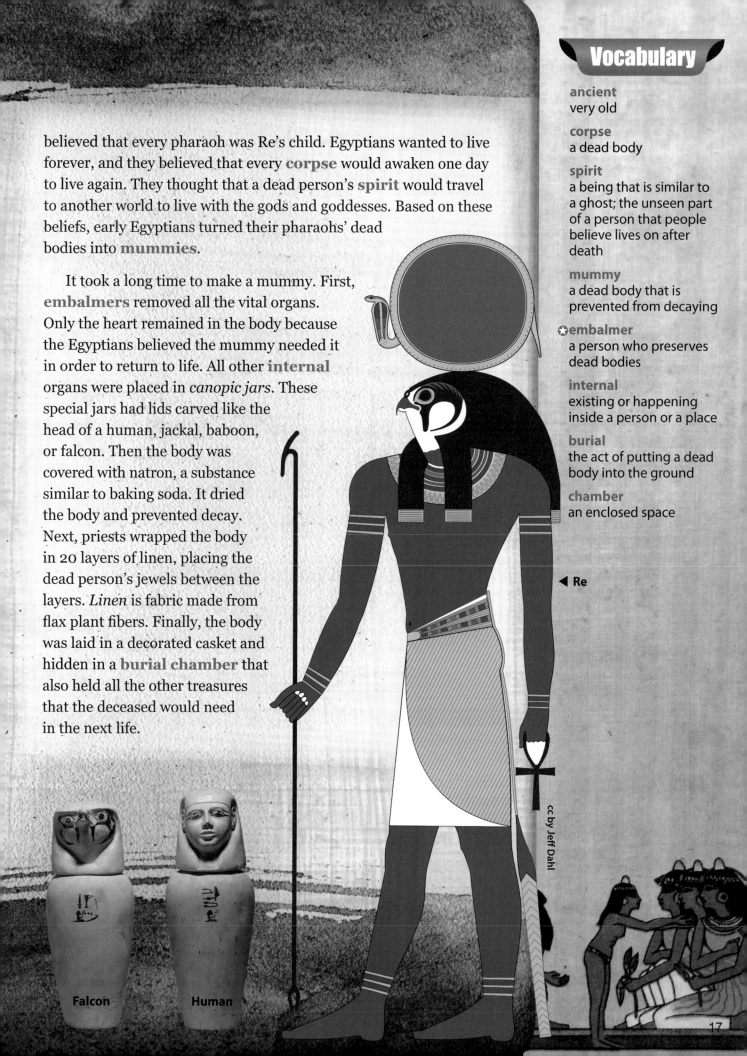

believed that every pharaoh was Re's child. Egyptians wanted to live forever, and they believed that every **corpse** would awaken one day to live again. They thought that a dead person's **spirit** would travel to another world to live with the gods and goddesses. Based on these beliefs, early Egyptians turned their pharaohs' dead bodies into **mummies**.

It took a long time to make a mummy. First, **embalmers** removed all the vital organs. Only the heart remained in the body because the Egyptians believed the mummy needed it in order to return to life. All other **internal** organs were placed in *canopic jars*. These special jars had lids carved like the head of a human, jackal, baboon, or falcon. Then the body was covered with natron, a substance similar to baking soda. It dried the body and prevented decay. Next, priests wrapped the body in 20 layers of linen, placing the dead person's jewels between the layers. *Linen* is fabric made from flax plant fibers. Finally, the body was laid in a decorated casket and hidden in a **burial chamber** that also held all the other treasures that the deceased would need in the next life.

**Falcon**  **Human**

◀ **Re**

cc by Jeff Dahl

cc by Jeff Dahl

## Vocabulary

**ancient**
very old

**corpse**
a dead body

**spirit**
a being that is similar to a ghost; the unseen part of a person that people believe lives on after death

**mummy**
a dead body that is prevented from decaying

⭐**embalmer**
a person who preserves dead bodies

**internal**
existing or happening inside a person or a place

**burial**
the act of putting a dead body into the ground

**chamber**
an enclosed space

17

# Reading Skills Comprehension Practice

**Part 1** Fill in the chart below with inferences that are based on clues from the passage.

| Inferences | Text Clues |
|---|---|
| **1.** Worshipping of gods and goddesses was a central element of Ancient Egyptian culture. | **1.** The ancient Egyptians had many gods. |
| **2.** _____ _____ | **2.** _____ _____ |
| **3.** _____ _____ | **3.** _____ _____ |

**Part 2** Think about any personal connections you can make to this passage. Write them below.

_____

_____

_____

**Part 3** Think about other topics or ideas that this passage reminds you of. Write your thoughts below.

_____

_____

_____

# Comprehension Review

**Fill in the best answer for each question.**

_____ ❶ The ancient Egyptians probably believed that _____ would be needed in the next life.
Ⓐ bread
Ⓑ jewels
Ⓒ the dead person's family
Ⓓ a boat

_____ ❷ What did the ancient Egyptians probably think the next life was like?
Ⓐ The ancient Egyptians did not believe in the next life.
Ⓑ People turned into animals.
Ⓒ People lived among the gods in a strange new world.
Ⓓ Jewels and other objects were not needed.

_____ ❸ How do you think the ancient Egyptians treated their pharaohs?
Ⓐ They did not respect them.
Ⓑ They treated their pharaohs like gods.
Ⓒ They treated their pharaohs much like they treated anyone else.
Ⓓ They did not have pharaohs.

_____ ❹ If you didn't know how to say _canopic_, what could you do?
Ⓐ read the title
Ⓑ read the rest of the passage
Ⓒ write the word
Ⓓ use a dictionary

_____ ❺ What was the _first_ step in turning a dead person into a mummy?
Ⓐ Embalmers would remove the vital organs.
Ⓑ The body was covered with natron.
Ⓒ The vital organs were placed in canopic jars.
Ⓓ Priests wrapped the body in 20 layers of linen.

_____ ❻ Which sentence is false?
Ⓐ The ancient Egyptians wanted to live forever.
Ⓑ Priests and embalmers prepared dead people to become mummies.
Ⓒ The ancient Egyptians burned their pharaohs when they died.
Ⓓ The ancient Egyptians believed in many gods.

# Word Power

**Choose the English word from the Vocabulary list that correctly matches the definition.**

 a dead body that is prevented from decaying
_____

 very old
_____

 an enclosed space
_____

 a person who preserves dead bodies
_____

### Reading Tip

- This is an advertisement for a sandwich shop.

- This passage contains relevant information about a new sandwich shop. However, depending on their purpose for reading, some people may find parts of the advertisement irrelevant.

# BUILD-YOUR-OWN SANDWICH SHOP

### Skill Overview

The main idea is the overall message of the author. It is the most important idea, or the central thought, that the author wants to convey. The main idea is often expressed directly, or it may be implied. The details are the pieces of information or evidence that support the main idea.

# THERE MUST BE 100 WAYS TO BUILD A SANDWICH . . . AND YOU CAN MAKE THEM ALL!

What makes a **delectable** sandwich? All the **ingredients** you like **stuffed** between two fluffy pieces of great-tasting bread!

At Build-Your-Own Sandwich Shop, you can **create** a sandwich exactly the way you want it. Choose from six fresh-baked breads and stuff them with more than 15 kinds of meat. Cover them with lettuce, tomatoes, onions, peppers, cheese—more than 30...count 'em...choices in all! And don't forget the **condiments**. What would a sandwich be without ketchup, mayonnaise, mustard, relish, salt, pepper, vinegar, and oil?

Our prices can't be **beat**. All 6-inch sandwiches are just $3.99. Foot-longs are just $6.99. Or make your own 6-foot Super Party Delight, which feeds a **dozen** people or more.

Eat it here or get it to go. For super savings, use our **coupon**!

## Build-Your-Own Sandwich Shop

## Vocabulary

**delectable**
delicious

**ingredient**
a substance that is combined with other things to make a dish or product

**stuff**
to push into and fill a space

**create**
to make something new, or invent something

**condiment**
something put on food to add flavor

**beat**
to defeat or do better than

**dozen**
group of 12

**coupon**
a piece of paper that can be used to get something for free or at a reduced price

**$3.99**
6-inch

**$6.99**
Foot-longs

# Reading Skills Comprehension Practice

**Part 1**  Write the main idea of this passage.

_____

_____

_____

_____

**Part 2**  Imagine that you are telling a stranger about the shop described in the passage. List the details that are relevant from your point of view and those that are not relevant.

| **Details That Are Relevant** | **Details That Are Not Relevant** |
|---|---|
| 1. You can choose the bread for your sandwich. | 1. You can eat your sandwich at the shop or take it to go. |
| 2. _____ | 2. _____ |
| 3. _____ | 3. _____ |

# Comprehension Review

**Fill in the best answer for each question.**

_____ ❶ **What is the most important thing the sandwich shop wants you to know?**
- Ⓐ You can create exactly the kind of sandwich you want.
- Ⓑ Foot-long sandwiches cost $6.99.
- Ⓒ You can eat in the shop or get your order to go.
- Ⓓ The shop has more than 15 kinds of meat.

_____ ❷ **Which detail does _not_ tell you about the sandwiches you can get?**
- Ⓐ Cover them with lettuce, tomatoes, onions, peppers, and cheese.
- Ⓑ Choose from six fresh-baked breads.
- Ⓒ Use our coupon!
- Ⓓ Stuff them with over 15 kinds of meat.

_____ ❸ **Which of these would be a good title for this passage?**
- Ⓐ New Sandwich Shop Closes
- Ⓑ New Sandwich Shop Builds Sandwiches Its Way
- Ⓒ Elegant New Dessert Shop Open
- Ⓓ New Sandwich Shop: Make It Your Way

_____ ❹ **_What makes a delectable sandwich? What does delectable mean?_**
- Ⓐ salty
- Ⓑ delicious
- Ⓒ rotten
- Ⓓ burned

_____ ❺ **What does the author want you to do?**
- Ⓐ buy a sandwich at the Build-Your-Own Sandwich Shop
- Ⓑ eat healthier foods
- Ⓒ learn how to cook
- Ⓓ learn about the history of sandwiches

_____ ❻ **What does a 6-foot Super Party Delight sandwich probably cost?**
- Ⓐ the same as a foot-long sandwich
- Ⓑ less than $3.99
- Ⓒ $3.99
- Ⓓ more than $6.99

# Word Power

**Choose the English word from the Vocabulary list that correctly matches the definition.**

**1**  something put on food to add flavor

_____

**2**  group of 12

_____

**3**  a piece of paper that can be used to get something for free or at reduced price

_____

**4**  delicious

_____

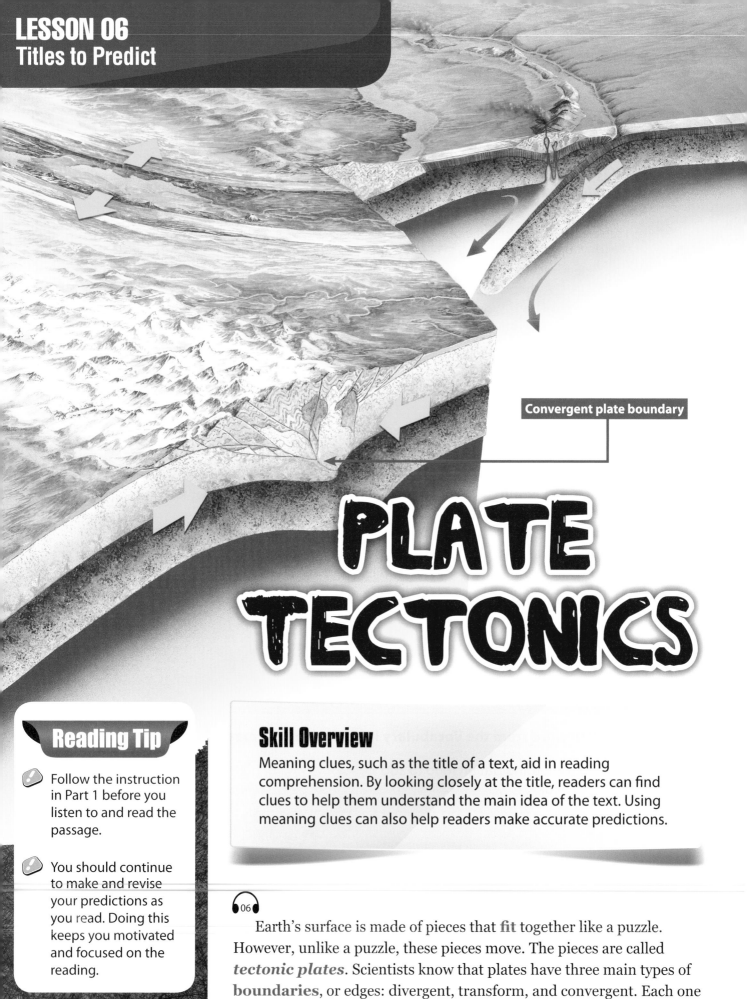

**Convergent plate boundary**

# PLATE TECTONICS

## Reading Tip

- Follow the instruction in Part 1 before you listen to and read the passage.

- You should continue to make and revise your predictions as you read. Doing this keeps you motivated and focused on the reading.

## Skill Overview

Meaning clues, such as the title of a text, aid in reading comprehension. By looking closely at the title, readers can find clues to help them understand the main idea of the text. Using meaning clues can also help readers make accurate predictions.

🎧 06

Earth's surface is made of pieces that **fit** together like a puzzle. However, unlike a puzzle, these pieces move. The pieces are called *tectonic plates*. Scientists know that plates have three main types of **boundaries**, or edges: divergent, transform, and convergent. Each one creates different land **features**.

**Divergent plate boundary**  **Transform plate boundary**

# DIVERGENT BOUNDARIES

The island of Iceland was made from the divergent boundary of a mid-ocean ridge. Here, two plates are moving away from each other very slowly—at a rate of two to four centimeters (one inch) per year. The **movement** of the plates causes magma to burst up through Earth's crust. This action forms volcanoes. Cooled material from these volcanic eruptions formed Iceland.

# TRANSFORM BOUNDARIES

Most transform boundaries are found in the ocean, but the San Andreas Fault is on land. The San Andreas Fault in California is a transform boundary. Two plates are sliding past each other instead of pulling away from each other. This sliding motion has caused major earthquakes all along the state's **coastline**.

# CONVERGENT BOUNDARIES

Plates can form convergent boundaries in one of three ways. Each type of convergent boundary has its own results. An ocean-ocean **collision** occurs between two ocean plates. Right now, the fast-moving Pacific Plate is crashing into the Filipino Plate. As the Pacific Plate **dives** into Earth's mantle, it melts, causing earthquakes and volcanoes. The arc-shaped Mariana Islands are underwater volcanoes that have grown large enough to rise above the water line.

In a continent-continent collision, two plates collide and then one plate subducts (moves under the other). The Himalayas are the result of a collision that started about 50 million years ago. The Indian and Eurasian plates crashed together to form the mountain range.

An ocean-continental collision is happening in South America right now. An oceanic plate is being subducted under a continental plate. This is why earthquakes and volcanoes are very common in Peru and Chile.

## Vocabulary

**fit**
to be the right size or shape for someone or something

**⊗tectonic plate**
a large piece of Earth's surface

**boundary**
an edge where two areas, such as tectonic plates, meet

**feature**
a typical quality or an important part of something

**movement**
a change of position

**coastline**
the particular shape of a coast

**collision**
a crash

**dive**
to move downward at an angle

cc by Luca Galuzzi

# Reading Skills Comprehension Practice

 **Make a prediction about the passage based on the title and headings.**

I think this passage will be about _____

_____

_____

 **After listening to and reading the passage, reread your prediction in Part 1. Compare your prediction with the actual content of the passage.**

My prediction was accurate! / My prediction was mostly correct, but . . . /
My prediction was wrong. The passage is actually about . . .

_____

_____

_____

**Part 3** **Explain how making predictions based on the title and headings helps you as a reader.**

Making predictions based on the title and headings helps me _____

_____

_____

Ridge

Divergent
plate
boundary

Convergent
plate
boundary

Earthquakes

Transform
plate
boundary

# Comprehension Review

**Fill in the best answer for each question.**

_____ ❶ The title tells you this passage is _mostly_ about _____

Ⓐ the planets.

Ⓑ pieces of Earth's surface called _tectonic plates_.

Ⓒ the newest volcanoes around the world.

Ⓓ the history of earthquakes.

_____ ❷ The headings are clues that this section is about _____

Ⓐ wildlife on our planet.

Ⓑ landforms in the United States.

Ⓒ how tectonic plates cause volcanoes.

Ⓓ different kinds of plate boundaries.

_____ ❸ What will you probably _not_ read about in this passage?

Ⓐ type of plate boundaries on other planets

Ⓑ the location of plate boundaries

Ⓒ how plate boundaries move

Ⓓ kinds of landforms caused by plate boundaries

_____ ❹ What caused the Himalayas?

Ⓐ a volcano

Ⓑ an ocean-ocean collision

Ⓒ a continent-continent collision

Ⓓ an earthquake

_____ ❺ The _____ is/are underwater volcanoes.

Ⓐ San Andreas Fault

Ⓑ Mariana Islands

Ⓒ Himalayas

Ⓓ Pacific Plate

_____ ❻ The San Andreas Fault has caused many _____

Ⓐ rivers.

Ⓑ volcanoes.

Ⓒ earthquakes.

Ⓓ convergent boundaries.

# Word Power

**Choose the English word from the Vocabulary list that correctly matches the definition.**

 a crash

_____

 an edge where two areas, such as tectonic plates, meet

_____

 a large piece of Earth's surface

_____

 the particular shape of a coast

_____

# Tuck Everlasting
# A Book Summary

## Reading Tip

- Follow the instructions in Parts 1 and 2 before you listen to and read the passage.

- This is a short summary of a book. A summary includes only highlights and leaves a lot of the information out.

## Skill Overview

Readers' selection of reading material helps **set a purpose for reading.** One should consider many factors when selecting reading material, including recommendations of others, personal interests, knowledge of authors, and text difficulty.

The Tuck family—Angus, Mae, Miles, and Jesse—have a strange and most **unusual** secret. They have looked the same for the past 87 years! One day, a young girl named Winnie Foster **accidentally** discovers 17-year-old Jesse and the source of their secret, a little bubbling **spring**. To keep Winnie from drinking the special water, the Tucks **kidnap** her and take her to their home.

The Tucks are gentle and kind to Winnie and fully intend to return her to her home the next day. Their only **concern** is that Winnie understands that living forever may not be the blessing that it seems. Pa Tuck tells Winnie about how it feels to be the same forever. He explains that to live means to constantly grow, move, and change and that part of changing includes dying. To him, his **existence** seems like nothing more than being a rock on the side of the road.

After hearing the Tucks' fantastic story, Winnie understands their concerns about her and what the **consequences** of drinking from the spring will be. Unfortunately, another stranger has overheard the whole story and plots to gain control of the spring in order to make his fortune by selling the water.

When the stranger's plans become clear to the Tucks, Mae accidentally kills him in her effort to stop him. Mae is put in jail by the constable, who has arrived just in time to witness the accident.

Winnie's compassion and belief in the Tucks lead her to help Mae escape. It is Winnie's way of making a difference in the world. The Tucks successfully escape, and Winnie is left to make the decision of her life—whether to drink from the spring when she turns 17 and join her beloved Jesse Tuck for **eternity**.

## Vocabulary

**unusual**
not normal or common

**accidentally**
by chance or by mistake

**spring**
a place where water naturally flows out from the ground

**kidnap**
to take a person away illegally by force

**concern**
a worried or nervous feeling about something

**existence**
the state of living or existing

**consequence**
something that happens as a result of a decision or an action

**eternity**
time that never ends or that has no limits

# Reading Skills Comprehension Practice

 **Answer the questions below regarding books you have read.**

**1.** What is your favorite book?

_____

**2.** Why is this book your favorite?

_____

_____

**3.** How do you choose what books to read?

_____

_____

 **Answer the questions below regarding your favorite author and interests in reading.**

**1.** Who is your favorite author? Why?

_____

**2.** What book of his/her have you recommended to someone else? Why?

_____

_____

**3.** Have your interests in reading materials changed over time? If so, how?

_____

_____

 **Tell whether you would like to read the book of Tuck Everlasting? Explain why or why not.**

_____

_____

_____

# Comprehension Review

**Fill in the best answer for each question.**

_____ ❶ **People who like to read _____ would enjoy the book *Tuck Everlasting.***
- Ⓐ fantasy novels
- Ⓑ cookbooks
- Ⓒ sports biographies
- Ⓓ home improvement guides

_____ ❷ **This would *not* be a good choice if you wanted to _____**
- Ⓐ read a novel.
- Ⓑ find out whether Winnie joins the Tuck family.
- Ⓒ think about what immortality might be like.
- Ⓓ read about how springs are formed.

_____ ❸ ***Tuck Everlasting* is a _____**
- Ⓐ collection of poems.
- Ⓑ biography.
- Ⓒ novel.
- Ⓓ user's manual.

_____ ❹ **What is a _constable_?**
- Ⓐ an officer who keeps the peace
- Ⓑ a firefighter
- Ⓒ a teacher
- Ⓓ a construction worker

_____ ❺ **What does Pa Tuck probably want Winnie to do?**
- Ⓐ He wants her to drink from the spring.
- Ⓑ He wants her to live forever.
- Ⓒ He wants her to tell everyone where the spring is.
- Ⓓ He wants her to choose not to drink from the spring.

_____ ❻ **Who wants to become rich by selling the spring water?**
- Ⓐ Mae Tuck
- Ⓑ the stranger
- Ⓒ Winnie Foster
- Ⓓ Jesse Tuck

# Word Power

**Choose the English word from the Vocabulary list that correctly matches the definition.**

 the state of living or existing

_____

 something that happens as a result of a decision or an action

_____

 not normal or common

_____

 time that never ends or that has no limits

_____

# Grandma-rama

## Skill Overview

The main character is the focus of a story. Learning how characters are developed (e.g., through their actions, physical descriptions, and character descriptions) can help readers understand how stories work and what message authors are trying to convey.

### Reading Tip

🔖 This passage describes one character, the narrator's grandma, in great detail, including her actions and motivations.

✏️ As you read and listen to the passage, underline the descriptive words and phrases the narrator uses to describe her grandma.

🎧 08

Most people have a picture in their minds of the perfect grandmother. She's a white-haired, sweet-faced, pleasantly plump homebody. Your basic garden-variety grandma is forever offering freshly baked cookies from her homey kitchen and **sage** advice from her rocking chair, right?

Not mine! My Grandma-rama is five feet two inches of pure energy and **adventure**. Forget the white hair—Gram decided on red, so red it is. She may be small, but don't be fooled by her size. Gram knows karate, and she isn't afraid to use it. Although she may look pint-sized, Gram is as **audacious** as they come.

Her apartment might as well not have a kitchen because Gram puts cooking way down on her **priority** list. I sometimes think wistfully of the grandmotherly types who would tempt me with homemade pies, cakes, and cookies. That would be one **traditional** grandmother trait that would come in handy. But Gram doesn't have time to cook. She's too busy traveling, taking classes, and trying new things.

At least once a year, Gram goes on an adventure vacation. She's seen lion prides and elephant herds in South Africa and has ridden a camel in the Gobi Desert. She's been deep-sea fishing off Mexico and has boated down the Amazon River. This year, she may take a whitewater **rafting** trip on the Colorado River or a trek on a **glacier** in Alaska.

And no napping by the fire on winter evenings, either. Gram says you're never too old to learn, and she's proving it by taking subjects like political science, filmmaking, and creative writing at the local college. She showed me the first chapter of her novel—I'm sworn to secrecy— and I think it's great! Of course, the detective is an older woman who looks much younger and has red hair.

Do I wish my grandmother made me chicken soup when I was sick? Told me entertaining stories of what life was like "long ago"? Cheered for every concert, sporting event, and school play? No way! It's more fun watching a grandmother who has a life and knows how to enjoy it. Instead of holding out for cookies and milk, I'm hoping for a **companion** ticket on that plane to Alaska with the one and only Grandma-rama!

## Vocabulary

**✪ sage**
wise

**adventure**
an unusual, exciting, and possibly dangerous activity

**✪ audacious**
willing to take risks

**priority**
something that is very important and must be dealt with before other things

**traditional**
following or based on customs or culture

**raft**
to travel or be transported in a flat rubber boat

**A raft**

**glacier**
a large piece of ice that moves slowly over land

**companion**
closely connected with something else

33

 **Part 1** Record the words and phrases the narrator uses to describe her grandma.

A **motivation** is a reason for doing something or behaving in a certain way; the motivation of characters often tell us a lot about them as people.

Descriptive Words or Phrases

five feet two inches

**Part 2** Describe the actions of the main character that tell us what she is really like.

_____

_____

_____

**Part 3** Describe the motivations of the narrator and her grandmother in the passage.

**The Narrator**

The motivation of the narrator is

_____

_____

_____

**The Grandmother**

The motivation of the grandmother is

_____

_____

_____

# Comprehension Review

**Fill in the best answer for each question.**

_____ **1** Which of these would be a good birthday present for Gram?
Ⓐ an apron
Ⓑ fuzzy slippers
Ⓒ yoga lessons
Ⓓ a cookbook

_____ **2** How might you describe Gram to someone who doesn't know her?
Ⓐ timid
Ⓑ adventurous
Ⓒ lazy
Ⓓ heavy

_____ **3** Gram would probably be _____ a trip to India.
Ⓐ bored by
Ⓑ angry about
Ⓒ afraid of
Ⓓ interested in

_____ **4** Which of these does Gram probably do well?
Ⓐ write
Ⓑ cook
Ⓒ sew
Ⓓ garden

_____ **5** The narrator is _____ Gram.
Ⓐ afraid of
Ⓑ proud of
Ⓒ embarrassed by
Ⓓ confused by

_____ **6** What kind of book is Gram writing?
Ⓐ a cookbook
Ⓑ a dictionary
Ⓒ a mystery
Ⓓ a travel book

# Word Power

**Choose the English word from the Vocabulary list that correctly matches the definition.**

**1**  closely connected with something else

_____

**2**  a large piece of ice that moves slowly over land

_____

**3**  wise

_____

**4**  an unusual, exciting, and possibly dangerous activity

_____

35

**A design for a flying machine (c. 1488), Institut de France, Paris**

**Anatomical study of the arm (c. 1510)**

# Leonardo da Vinci: Inventor

## Skill Overview

Authors organize the information in their writing so that it makes sense to readers. They may choose to write information in a logical order based on the topic. Recognition of this text structure aids comprehension.

**Leonardo da Vinci**

## Da Vinci's Accomplishments

Leonardo da Vinci is one of the most famous artists the world has ever known, but he is also celebrated for his many **inventions**. His detailed notebooks contain several sketches and drawings. These are accompanied by odd-looking handwriting (words written backward to confuse the uninvited reader). His notebooks **outlined** plans for ideas that were four centuries ahead of their time. His inventions ranged from flying machines to weapons to a **device** for roasting pigs. In **intricate** drawings, Leonardo showed how alarm clocks, parachutes, diving suits, and submarines might be constructed. He created **blueprints** for the chain drive used on bicycles today. Other designs were for machines that could make coins, screws, cloth, and rope. Most of his ideas were never actually built. However, history has shown that he was definitely a man ahead of his time.

## Da Vinci's Life

Leonardo da Vinci was born on April 15, 1452, in a hilltop city called *Vinci*. He was raised by his stepmother. His mother, Caterina, had been unable to bring a dowry to the marriage, so his father, Ser Piero da Vinci, married a young woman of great wealth. As a child, Leonardo was **fascinated** with nature. He liked to study birds as he walked through the Tuscan hills near his home. Later in life, he would often buy caged birds just so he could free them. He had a great respect for all living creatures.

*The Last Supper*

By the age of 10, Leonardo was living with his family in Florence, Italy. Here, he was a student in artist Verrocchio's studio, where he studied for the next 10 years. It was during his stay in Milan that he painted *The Last Supper* and the *Mona Lisa*. Unable to continue making a living there, Leonardo began moving from place to place. He worked as an **engineer** and mapmaker for the Pope. He also worked as an engineer for the French governors of Milan and as a member of the papal court.

Finally, in 1516, the king of France, Francis I, invited Leonardo to live there. Leonardo started a new life. As the king's official painter and architect, Leonardo planned a new castle for Francis I and oversaw its construction. He also designed a **network** of canals that would be installed some 300 years later.

When Leonardo da Vinci died on May 2, 1519, the world lost a great man. However, his many ideas and inventions would bring him new life when they were rediscovered by Napoleon some 200 years later.

## Vocabulary

**invention**
something that has never been made before

**outline**
to describe the most important parts of something

**device**
an object designed to do a specific thing

✪**intricate**
having a lot of detail

✪**blueprint**
an early plan or design that explains how something might be achieved

**fascinate**
to interest someone a lot

**engineer**
a person whose job is to design or build machines, engines, or things such as roads and railways.

**network**
a system of roads, freeways, waterways, etc., that connect to one another

# Reading Skills Comprehension Practice

**Part 1** Think about a book you read that was written in a logical order. Share your ideas about the book and how it was organized.

> Manuals are generally presented in a logical order. I read a stereo manual last night . . .

**Part 2** Answer questions about Leonardo da Vinci based on the passage.

**1.** When was Leonardo da Vinci born?

**2.** What were some of his childhood interests?

**3.** What did he do during his stay in Milan?

**4.** Why is Leonardo da Vinci considered a great man?

**Part 3** Match the text description on the left with the appropriate organizational structure on the right. Write the corresponding letter on the line. Some organizational structures are used more than once.

| Texts | Organizational Structures |
|---|---|
| _____ **1.** phone book | **A.** similar items are grouped together |
| _____ **2.** a book about the history of Mexico | **B.** alphabetical order |
| _____ **3.** catalog of music CDs and instruments | **C.** compare and contrast |
| _____ **4.** directions for making a birdhouse | **D.** sequential order |
| _____ **5.** book about different wars | **E.** chronological order |
| _____ **6.** index | **F.** proposition and support |
| _____ **7.** letter to the editor of a newspaper | |
| _____ **8.** article about methods of transportation | |
| _____ **9.** a biography of Abraham Lincoln | |
| _____ **10.** recipe | |

# Comprehension Review

**Fill in the best answer for each question.**

_____ ❶ **Leonardo studied with Verrocchio** *after* _____
- Ⓐ he studied birds.
- Ⓑ he painted the *Mona Lisa*.
- Ⓒ he worked as an engineer and mapmaker.
- Ⓓ he became the king's official painter and architect.

_____ ❷ *Before* **Leonardo started a new life in France, he** _____
- Ⓐ designed a network of canals in France.
- Ⓑ planned a new castle.
- Ⓒ worked as an engineer for the French governors of Milan.
- Ⓓ became the king's official painter and architect.

_____ ❸ *After* **Leonardo died, what was rediscovered by Napoleon 300 years later?**
- Ⓐ the *Mona Lisa*
- Ⓑ Leonardo's ideas and inventions
- Ⓒ Leonardo's wealth
- Ⓓ Leonardo's designs for canals in France

_____ ❹ **What caused Leonardo to start moving from place to place?**
- Ⓐ He didn't get along with his family.
- Ⓑ His art took him all over the world.
- Ⓒ He couldn't stay in one place.
- Ⓓ He was unable to make a living in Milan.

_____ ❺ **Besides the *Mona Lisa*, which other famous painting did Leonardo da Vinci paint?**
- Ⓐ *The Last Supper*
- Ⓑ *Starry Night*
- Ⓒ *Water Lilies*
- Ⓓ *The Tragedy*

_____ ❻ **People who enjoy reading about _____ would probably like this passage.**
- Ⓐ world literature
- Ⓑ nature
- Ⓒ Tuscany
- Ⓓ art history

# Word Power

**Choose the English word from the Vocabulary list that correctly matches the definition.**

 **1** having a lot of detail

_____

 **2** a system of roads, freeways, waterways, etc., that connect to one another

_____

 **3** an object designed to do a specific thing

_____

 **4** to describe the most important parts of something

_____

# Taking a Sample

## Reading Tip

- Follow the instructions in Parts 1 and 2 before you listen to and read the passage.

- Pay close attention to the headings in this lesson.

## Skill Overview

Headings help readers determine the main idea and locate information in a text. Often, headings state the topic in a single word or short phrase. Learning to recognize headings and using them consistently will help readers to increase reading comprehension.

## 🎧10 Problem

Tamika, Alejandro, and Shana are running on the same ticket for president, vice president, and treasurer of their middle school. They all think they have a good chance of winning if a large number of students **vote** next week. The **candidates** decide to **conduct** a **survey** to see how many students plan on voting in the school **election**. Each of the three conducts a different type of survey. Which of their **predictions** for voter turnout is likely the most **accurate**?

# Students Who Plan to Vote Next Week

| Method of Picking the Sample | Prediction Based on Survey Results |
| --- | --- |
| Tamika asked 45 of her friends. | 90% of the students will vote |
| Alejandro put the names of all seventh graders in a bowl, picked 60 names at random, and asked those students. | 75% of the students will vote |
| Shana put the names of all the students in the school in a bowl, picked 60 names at random, and asked those students. | 55% of the students will vote |

**Vocabulary**

**vote**
to express your choice or opinion, especially by officially writing a mark on a paper or by raising your hand

**candidate**
a person who runs for a political office or position

**conduct**
to organize and perform a particular activity

**survey**
an examination of opinions, behaviors, etc., made by asking people questions

**election**
a time when people vote in order to choose someone for a political or official job

**prediction**
a statement about what you think will happen in the future

**accurate**
correct

**biased**
unfairly preferring one thing or person over another thing or person

## Solution

### 1. Tamika's Sample

Her sample includes only friends. This is a *convenience sample*, which is the easiest to gather. But Tamika's friends probably don't represent all the students at the school. They will vote for her because they want to support her. This is called a *biased sample* because it is not representative of the entire population.

### 2. Alejandro's Sample

His sample is a random selection of seventh grade students. All the seventh grade students have the same chance of being selected. But he is polling only seventh grade students. They may not represent the other grade levels, so his sample may be **biased** as well.

### 3. Shana's Sample

This random sample came from the entire school population. Shana's sample will probably represent the entire school. Her sample is the least biased, so it is most likely to accurately predict what will happen next week.

## Conclusion

About 55% of the school's students will likely vote next week.

# Reading Skills Comprehension Practice

**Part 1** Describe a time when you used headings to help you understand something you were reading.

> _(blank lines)_

**Part 2** Write your predictions about each section based on the headings.

| Headings | Predictions |
|---|---|
| **Problem** | I think this section is about |
| **Students Who Plan to Vote Next Week** | I think this section is about |
| **Solution** | I think this section is about |
| **Conclusion** | I think this section is about |

**Part 3** Write the main idea of this passage in the space below.

> _(blank lines)_

# Comprehension Review

**Fill in the best answer for each question.**

_____ ❶ **Where will you find the problem described in this passage?**

Ⓐ before the title

Ⓑ under the first heading

Ⓒ in the box

Ⓓ at the end of the passage

_____ ❷ *Tamika's Sample*

**This heading tells you that the section gives details about**

_____

Ⓐ the kind of sample that Tamika took.

Ⓑ how Alejandro conducted his survey.

Ⓒ how to conduct a survey.

Ⓓ whether middle school students vote in elections.

_____ ❸ **Which detail does *not* belong in the table?**

Ⓐ percentage of students predicted to vote

Ⓑ method of obtaining a sample

Ⓒ definition of *sample*

Ⓓ how many students were sampled

_____ ❹ *Tamika, Alejandro, and Shana are running on the same ticket for president, vice president, and treasurer of their middle school.*

**What does *ticket* mean in this sentence?**

Ⓐ admission to an event

Ⓑ a fine for speeding

Ⓒ the sound a clock makes

Ⓓ a list of people running for office

_____ ❺ **Why is Tamika's sample called a *convenience sample*?**

Ⓐ It is the most accurate kind of sample.

Ⓑ It is the easiest to get.

Ⓒ It is the hardest to get.

Ⓓ It represents the whole population.

_____ ❻ **What advice would you give Tamika, Alejandro, and Shana to help them win?**

Ⓐ Wait until next year to run for election.

Ⓑ Try to talk people out of voting.

Ⓒ Don't do anything; you will probably win.

Ⓓ Try to get more people to vote.

# Word Power

**Choose the English word from the Vocabulary list that correctly matches the definition.**

**1** correct

_____

**2** unfairly preferring one thing or person over another thing or person

_____

**3** a person who runs for a political office or position

_____

**4** a time when people vote in order to choose someone for a political or official job

_____

# Newton's Laws of Motion

## Skill Overview

A **topic sentence** is a general sentence that expresses the main idea of a paragraph. It is usually the first sentence in the paragraph and is followed by supporting sentences. Recognizing topic sentences can help readers make meaningful predictions about the content of a text.

### Reading Tip

- Follow the instructions in Parts 1 and 2 before you listen to and read the passage.

- The passage is divided into four sections. The introductory paragraph is followed by four paragraphs about Newton's Laws. Each section has a topic sentence.

🎧 11

Isaac Newton is perhaps most famous for three laws about objects in motion and the forces that act upon them. Newton didn't write the laws as we know them today; other scientists studying Newton's work wrote them and called them Newton's laws of motion. Newtonian mechanics are based on the laws of motion.

Inertia keeps this bicycle going straight until the rider turns.

## Newton's First Law

Newton's first law of motion concerns **inertia**. *Inertia* is the **resistance** to changes in motion. It has a significant effect on objects in motion. The law says that as long as an unbalanced force doesn't **interfere**, an object will keep doing what it's already doing. This law applies to objects whether they are still or moving. Objects that are still remain still. Objects that are moving continue moving with a constant **velocity**, or speed.

## Newton's Second Law

Newton's second law of motion concerns *acceleration*. It describes the effect of applying a force to an object. It says that the greater the force, the more the object **accelerates**, or changes velocity. Additionally, the object will always move in the same direction as the force. A greater force is needed to make a heavy object accelerate the same rate as a light object. This makes sense. For example, a bowling ball is more difficult to throw than a tennis ball. It is more difficult to stop a car than a bicycle.

**A great force is needed to make a heavy bowling ball accelerate.**

## Newton's Third Law

Newton's third law of motion concerns *action* and *reaction*. It says that for every action, there is an **equal** and **opposite reaction**. This means that whenever a force pushes on an object, the object pushes back in the opposite direction. The force of the object pushing back is called the *reaction force*.

This law explains why a rowboat moves when oarsmen row. The oarsmen push backward on the water with an oar. The water pushes back on the oar with an equal and opposite reaction. This moves the boat forward. It also explains why an armchair sits on the floor instead of crashing through it: The floor pushes against the chair and keeps it there. Alternatively, when you hit a tennis ball with a racquet, the ball has an equal and opposite reaction. Hit it just right, and all that force creates a killer serve!

**Hitting a tennis ball and pulling oars cause an equal and opposite reaction.**

## Vocabulary

**inertia**
resistance to changes in motion

**resistance**
the act of fighting or the force that goes against something

**interfere**
to become involved in something

**velocity**
the speed of movement

**accelerate**
to move faster

**equal**
the same in amount, number, or size

**opposite**
completely different

**reaction**
a behavior, feeling or action that is a direct result of something else

# Reading Skills Comprehension Practice

 Write your predictions about this passage based on the topic sentence of the first paragraph: "Isaac Newton is perhaps most famous for three laws about objects in motion and the forces that act upon them."

I think this passage will be about

_____

_____

 **Part 2** Write the topic sentences for each section below.

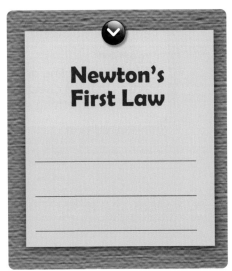

### Newton's First Law

_____

_____

### Newton's Second Law

_____

_____

### Newton's Third Law

_____

_____

**Part 3** Indicate whether your prediction in Part 1 was accurate. Explain why or why not.

My prediction was

_____

_____

# Comprehension Review

**Fill in the best answer for each question.**

**❶** *Newton is perhaps most famous for three laws about objects in motion and the forces that act upon them.*

**What does this sentence indicate the passage will be about?**

Ⓐ the newest discoveries about the solar system

Ⓑ Newton's life in England

Ⓒ Newton's three laws

Ⓓ where to go to buy books about Newton

**❷** *"Newton's Second Law"*

**Which detail will you probably *not* find in this section?**

Ⓐ information about the first law

Ⓑ information about acceleration

Ⓒ how the second law works

Ⓓ an example of the second law

**❸** *Inertia is the resistance to changes in motion.*

**Which topic sentence matches this detail?**

Ⓐ Newton's third law of motion concerns action and reaction.

Ⓑ Newton's second law concerns acceleration.

Ⓒ Newton's first law of motion concerns inertia.

Ⓓ This law explains why a rowboat moves when oarsmen row.

**❹ If you didn't know how to pronounce *inertia*, what should you do?**

Ⓐ write the word

Ⓑ use a dictionary

Ⓒ spell the word

Ⓓ reread the title

**❺** *Objects that are moving continue moving with a constant velocity.*

**What is another word for *velocity*?**

Ⓐ appearance

Ⓑ sound

Ⓒ color

Ⓓ speed

**❻ What is the purpose of this passage?**

Ⓐ to explain Newton's Laws of Motion

Ⓑ to tell about Newton's life

Ⓒ to get readers to buy a bicycle

Ⓓ to teach readers how to row a boat

# Word Power

**Choose the English word from the Vocabulary list that correctly matches the definition.**

**1**  resistance to changes in motion

_____

**2**  to become involved in something

_____

**3**  the speed of movement

_____

**4**  to move faster

_____

### Reading Tip

Follow the instruction in Part1 after you listen to and read the first paragraph.

# Twilight

## Skill Overview

Literary devices are specific aspects of writing that help readers understand and decode meaning in a text. These devices include **personification**, **simile**, **metaphor**, **alliteration**, **foreshadowing**, **suspense**, and **tone**.

Have you ever witnessed a scene of such **tranquility** that its beauty **overwhelmed** you? Such was the scene of two beautiful deer **grazing** in the still pasture as twilight approached. Pinks, yellows, and oranges **streaked** the sky like a magnificent painting. Every few seconds, one of the deer's tails twitched as it lifted its head to look around carefully before returning to its dinner. Dark shadows lengthened as the evening crept closer and closer. The forest that surrounded the pasture seemed to beckon the deer, urging them to seek refuge from any lurking dangers.

Suddenly, from out of the forest, a large fox raced toward the deer. As soon as they sensed movement, the deer took off in opposite directions, at first **erratic** and **confused**, then purposeful and focused as they ran to evade their predator. The fox paused. Then, **instinctively**, it raced after the slower deer deep into the pine forest. Then, all was quiet again in the pasture. Quiet. Dark. Somehow less peaceful.

The sky quickly became a murky grayish pink. The sky painting appeared as if a bucket of water had spilled across the canvas, washing away the vibrant colors. Two rabbits darted playfully, and fireflies flickered in the **dusk**. Within minutes, the atmosphere of peace had returned, the skirmish toward death forgotten.

## Vocabulary

**tranquility**
the quality of being free from disturbance

**overwhelm**
to cause someone to feel sudden strong emotion

**graze**
to eat grass

**streak**
to make long, thin noticeable lines of a different color

**erratic**
not following a consistent pattern of behavior

**confused**
unable to think clearly or to understand something

**instinctively**
acting according to natural behaviors that have not been learned

**dusk**
the time before night when it is not yet dark

49

# Reading Skills Comprehension Practice

 *power up*

| **Foreshadowing** suggests something is going to happen in a story. | A **suspenseful moment** in a story occurs when readers feel excitement and uncertainty about how the story will progress or end. | **Figurative language** includes simile, metaphor, personification, and alliteration. |
|---|---|---|

**Part 1** Tell how the author uses **foreshadowing** in the first paragraph.

The author uses foreshadowing by _____

_____

_____

**Part 2** Describe a **suspenseful moment** in the story.

A suspenseful moment occurs in the story when _____

_____

_____

**Part 3** In the table below, record three examples of **figurative language** used in the passage.

| Figurative Language | | | |
|---|---|---|---|
| 1. the evening crept closer | 2. | 3. | 4. |

# Comprehension Review

**Fill in the best answer for each question.**

_____ ❶ *Pinks, yellows, and oranges streaked the sky like a magnificent painting.*
**What is this an example of?**
Ⓐ metaphor
Ⓑ simile
Ⓒ personification
Ⓓ alliteration

_____ ❷ **Which is an example of personification?**
Ⓐ The fox paused.
Ⓑ Suddenly, from out of the forest, a large fox raced toward the deer.
Ⓒ Then, all was quiet again in the pasture.
Ⓓ The forest that surrounded the pasture seemed to beckon to the deer, urging them to seek refuge from any lurking dangers.

_____ ❸ **Which is a good example of alliteration?**
Ⓐ tails twitched
Ⓑ opposite directions
Ⓒ painting appeared
Ⓓ skirmish toward death

_____ ❹ **At what time do the events in the passage probably take place?**
Ⓐ 9:00 a.m.
Ⓑ midnight
Ⓒ 6:30 p.m.
Ⓓ noon

_____ ❺ **What causes the deer to run away?**
Ⓐ rabbits
Ⓑ a sudden thunderstorm
Ⓒ hunters
Ⓓ a fox

_____ ❻ **The events described in the passage probably take place in a _____**
Ⓐ desert.
Ⓑ forest.
Ⓒ backyard.
Ⓓ big city.

# Word Power

**Choose the English word from the Vocabulary list that correctly matches the definition.**

 not following a consistent pattern of behavior
_____

 the time before night when it is not yet dark
_____

 the quality of being free from disturbance
_____

 acting according to natural behaviors that have not been learned
_____

51

# THE UNSINKABLE TITANIC

## Skill Overview
Cause and effect is a pattern that explains the result of an event or occurrence and the reasons it happened. Successful readers can identify this pattern and can use appropriate strategies to better understand the text.

## Reading Tip

Follow the instruction in Part 1 before you listen to and read the passage.

**Edward J. Smith, captain of the Titanic**

In April 1912, a new luxury liner was ready for its maiden **voyage**. The *Titanic* had the best of everything, and only the elite could afford first-class passage. Some paid more than $4,000 for the trip, while many of the crew did not earn even $1,000 in a year. Many famous people were on board, including millionaire John Jacob Astor and his wife, and Isidor and Ida Straus, wealthy department store owners.

The ship's promoters claimed that their **vessel** was unsinkable. Its **hull** had 16 watertight compartments. Even if two compartments flooded, the ship would still float. In general, the passengers were confident that the ship had the best design and latest technology.

Late on the night of April 14, the *Titanic* was sailing in the North Atlantic Ocean on its trip from England to New York City. The ship was traveling at nearly top speed. With **icebergs** in the area, the ship's speed was far too fast. At 11:40 p.m., the *Titanic* rubbed against an iceberg for about 10 seconds. Unfortunately, the hull of the ship

Mrs. John Jacob Astor

was made of a type of steel that became brittle in the icy waters of the North Atlantic. As a result, several small cracks appeared, and seams came apart. Water started to pour inside, making the hull weaker.

Six distress **signals** were sent out right away. Another ship, the *California*, was just 20 minutes away at the time. No one there heard the signal because its radio operator was not on duty. The *California* was about four hours away, and it did respond. However, when the *California* arrived at 4:00 a.m., it was too late for many passengers. Just after 2:00 a.m., water had flooded through the hull to the ship's bow. This caused the entire vessel to split in two.

At first, the passengers aboard the ship were calm. They had expected to reach lifeboats with ease and then be **rescued** by other ships. They did not know that the *Titanic*'s lifeboats had room for only about 1,200 people. That was far fewer than the number of people on board. When people saw how **dire** the situation was, many stepped aside for younger passengers to board lifeboats. Among these heroes were the Astors, the Strauses, and Captain Edward J. Smith. In all, 705 people survived the wreck—most of them women and children. The other 1,517 died in the icy North Atlantic waters.

In 1985, a team of scientists found the **wreckage** of the *Titanic*. People had thought that the iceberg had ripped a large gash in the boat, causing it to sink. However, scientists were able to prove that the steel hull and the ship's high speed were to blame for the tragedy.

John Jacob Astor

Isidor Straus

## Vocabulary

**voyage**
a long journey, especially by ship

**vessel**
a boat or ship

**hull**
the frame of a ship or boat

**iceberg**
a very large mass of ice that floats in the sea

**signal**
an action, movement, or sound that gives information, a message, or a warning

**rescue**
to help someone or something out of a dangerous situation

**dire**
causing great fear or suffering

**wreckage**
a badly damaged object or the separated parts of a badly damaged object

# Reading Skills Comprehension Practice

 Think of two things you have done today that show a cause-and-effect relationship. Write them below.

| Cause | Effect |
|---|---|
| **1** I didn't study for my test. | **1** I did poorly on my test. |
| **2** | **2** |
| **3** | **3** |

 Write words or phrases from the passage that show it is written in a cause-and-effect pattern.

As a result

 Record two examples of cause and effect in the passage.

| Cause | Effect |
|---|---|
| **1** The Titanic rubbed against an iceberg for about 10 seconds. | **1** Small cracks appeared in the hull, and water started to pour inside. |
| **2** | **2** |
| **3** | **3** |

# Comprehension Review

**Fill in the best answer for each question.**

**❶ What was the effect of the cracks in the *Titanic*'s hull?**

Ⓐ Water poured inside, making the hull weaker.

Ⓑ The ship's promoters claimed that their vessel was unsinkable.

Ⓒ The ship was traveling at nearly top speed.

Ⓓ At 11:40 p.m., the *Titanic* rubbed against an iceberg for about 10 seconds.

**❷ In the end, scientists determined that _____ caused the *Titanic* to sink.**

Ⓐ an iceberg

Ⓑ the *Carpathia*

Ⓒ the steel hull and the ship's high speed

Ⓓ the large number of people on board

**❸ What caused the hull of the ship to crack after it rubbed against the iceberg?**

Ⓐ The *Titanic* was too crowded.

Ⓑ The steel hull became brittle in icy waters.

Ⓒ Water started to pour inside.

Ⓓ The seams in the steel hull came apart.

**❹ Why didn't the *California* respond to the *Titanic*?**

Ⓐ The waters of the North Atlantic were too cold.

Ⓑ The *California* had already sunk.

Ⓒ It was too far away.

Ⓓ Its radio operator was not on duty.

**❺ Which statement is *not* true?**

Ⓐ Most of the passengers on the *Titanic* died in the North Atlantic Ocean.

Ⓑ The ship was traveling far too fast.

Ⓒ Most people could afford passage on the *Titanic*.

Ⓓ The *California* did not respond to the *Titanic*'s distress signals.

**❻ People who enjoy reading about _____ would enjoy this passage.**

Ⓐ history

Ⓑ animals

Ⓒ famous authors

Ⓓ computers

# Word Power

**Choose the English word from the Vocabulary list that correctly matches the definition.**

 the frame of a ship or boat

_____

 causing great fear or suffering

_____

 a boat or ship

_____

 a badly damaged object or the separated parts of a badly damaged object

_____

mantle

outer core

inner
core

# Earth's Structure

## Skill Overview

**Paraphrasing** information in text means to put an author's words into one's own words. This allows readers to repeat ideas in an original way, which helps them to deepen their understanding of what has been read.

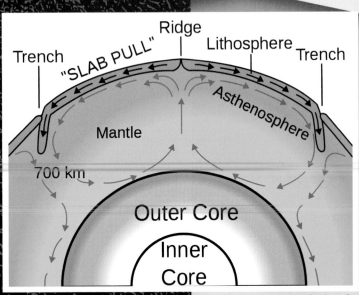

Trench "SLAB PULL" Ridge Lithosphere Trench

Asthenosphere

Mantle

700 km

Outer Core

Inner Core

cc by Surachit

🎧14
Have you ever wondered how Earth is put together? Most people live their lives without thinking about the planet under their feet. Some people do. They wonder about Earth; they **investigate** it, theorize about it, and explore it. These people are **geologists**, and they study Earth and how it is structured. They have **discovered** a number of interesting things.

## For "Eggsample"

Imagine Earth as a hard-boiled egg: An egg has a shell and Earth has a **crust**; an egg has liquid inside its shell and Earth has hot magma under its crust. If Earth were an egg, it would be a 6,400-kilometer (3,977-mile) trip from its shell (the crust) down to its center!

We live on Earth's crust, the cooled and hardened outer shell of the planet. All the continents of Earth are a part of the crust, and so is the ocean floor.

Just like a cracked eggshell, Earth's crust is cracked into multiple pieces. If you look at the edges of the continents, you might notice that they look like cracks on an eggshell. Earth also has other **layers** beneath the crust. They are the *mantle* and the *outer* and *inner cores*. These layers are made of *magma*, or molten rock, and their temperatures range from hundreds to thousands of degrees Fahrenheit.

## Recycling Crust

Molten magma rises to the surface through cracks in Earth's crust; when it cools, it creates new crust. This implies that there is more crust on Earth's surface today than there was millions of years ago. However, that can't be right, so geologists have a theory to explain this **phenomenon**.

If Earth oozes molten magma in one place, then it must reabsorb crust somewhere else. Sure enough, studies have revealed that the Atlantic Ocean floor is **expanding** and the Pacific Ocean floor is shrinking. New crust has been made in the Atlantic Ocean, and old crust has been destroyed in the Pacific.

Geologists found that the Pacific Ocean floor dives down into deep **trenches** under continents. These trenches are called *subduction zones*. The expanding and shrinking ocean floors are an example of how Earth is really a recycler. Rocks are created and later recycled. Proof of recycled rocks comes from mapping of earthquakes and volcanoes. Most of these rocks are found near undersea ridges and subduction zones.

### Vocabulary

**investigate**
to examine something carefully

**geologist**
a scientist who studies rocks and soil to learn about Earth's history and early life

**discover**
to find information, a place, or an object

**crust**
the hard outer covering of something

**layer**
a level of material that lies under or over another level

**phenomenon**
an event that can be observed in society or in nature, often rare or significant

**expand**
to increase in size, number

**trench**
a long and narrow hole in the ocean floor, usually with steep sides

# Reading Skills Comprehension Practice

**Part 1** Review the passage and think about the beginning, middle, and end. Write a **summary** for each part of the passage.

**Part 2** Use the 5W and H questions to write a second draft of your paraphrased version of the passage below.

**Part 3** Write the main idea of the passage.

# Comprehension Review

**Fill in the best answer for each question.**

_____ ❶ **Which sentence best paraphrases the information about Earth's structure in the passage?**
- Ⓐ Earth has a shell with cracks in it.
- Ⓑ Earth also has other layers beneath the crust: the mantle and the outer and inner core.
- Ⓒ We live on Earth's crust.
- Ⓓ Like an egg, Earth has a shell and a center.

_____ ❷ **Which sentence best paraphrases the first paragraph?**
- Ⓐ Some people wonder about Earth.
- Ⓑ Geologists have made some very interesting discoveries about Earth.
- Ⓒ Have you ever wondered how Earth is put together?
- Ⓓ Some people investigate Earth.

_____ ❸ **Which sentence best explains how Earth's crust is recycled?**
- Ⓐ Magma oozes out on the floor of the Atlantic Ocean, and the crust is destroyed in the Pacific Ocean.
- Ⓑ Magma oozes out on the floor of the Atlantic Ocean.
- Ⓒ Earth's crust is recycled.
- Ⓓ Volcanoes and earthquakes appear near subduction zones.

_____ ❹ **Which is _not_ a layer under Earth's crust?**
- Ⓐ mantle
- Ⓑ inner core
- Ⓒ continent
- Ⓓ outer core

_____ ❺ **Which is part of Earth's crust?**
- Ⓐ inner core
- Ⓑ continent
- Ⓒ outer core
- Ⓓ mantle

_____ ❻ **Why did the author likely write this passage?**
- Ⓐ to convince readers to become geologists
- Ⓑ to give an opinion about geologists
- Ⓒ to teach readers how to make a volcano
- Ⓓ to teach about Earth's structure

# Word Power

**Choose the English word from the Vocabulary list that correctly matches the definition.**

 a scientist who studies rocks and soil to learn about Earth's history and early life

_____

 a long, narrow hole in the ocean floor, usually with steep sides

_____

 an event that can be observed in society or in nature, often rare or significant

_____

 a level of material that lies under or over another level

_____

# Lake Erie's Struggle to Survive

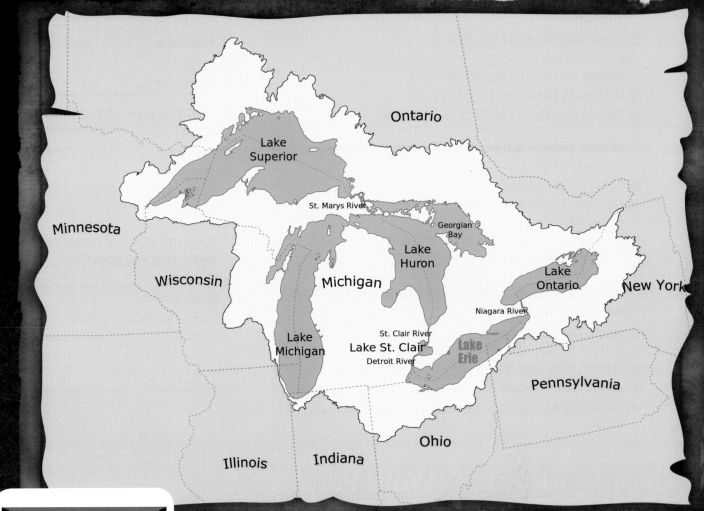

Ontario

Lake
Superior

St. Marys River

Georgian
Bay

Minnesota

Lake
Huron

Lake
Ontario

Wisconsin

Michigan

New York

Niagara River

St. Clair River

Lake
Michigan

Lake St. Clair

Lake
Erie

Detroit River

Pennsylvania

Illinois

Indiana

Ohio

## Reading Tip

- Follow the instructions in Parts 1 and 2 before you listen to and read the passage.

- Different typefaces are used within the passage, including in the **title**, **headings**, and **captions**.

- Typeface can help you determine the main idea of a text.

## Skill Overview

**Typeface** is the style and size of letters. There are many font sizes and styles, including *italic*, **colored**, and **boldface** print. Authors use different typefaces to organize information and to emphasize important words and ideas.

🎧 15

    America and Canada share an important **natural resource** called the *Great Lakes*, which hold one-fifth of the world's freshwater. These five lakes are so large that they can be seen from outer space.

# POLLUTING LAKE ERIE

From the mid-1800s to the mid-1900s, cities and farms **dumped** untreated waste into Lake Erie, one of the Great Lakes. The people believed that the lake was so big that all of the waste and chemicals would be **diluted** into insignificance. Although all of the Great Lakes **suffered** from pollution, Lake Erie suffered the most **damage** because of its warm temperature and shallow depth. By the late 1960s, the lake was so **foul** that most of its fish had died. The high bacteria count made the water unsafe for swimming. The lake stunk from algae overgrowth. Mats of green slime floated on its surface. Its **condition** was so bad that scientists called Lake Erie "dead."

# SAVING LAKE ERIE

In 1972, the Canadian and American governments agreed to clean up the lake. After they found that the lake's worst enemy was the phosphate in laundry soap, people protested until the soap makers removed this chemical. New laws required waste to go through a **treatment** plant before entering the lake. The two nations spent $8 billion to help clean Lake Erie.

After 10 years, the quality of Lake Erie's water had improved so much that it could be restocked with fish and people could once again swim in it. Even so, more must be done to protect the lake and keep its water clean. Recently, scientists were alarmed to discover a "dead zone" in the lake. In this dead zone, the lake has low levels of oxygen and no living things—except for algae. Even outside the dead zone, more than 300 chemicals still pollute the lake to some degree. This causes problems for wildlife. For example, ospreys have such thin eggshells that few of their young hatch. Male whitefish do not develop normally. Scientists are doing research to determine how to solve these problems and make the lake as nature intended it.

The worst algal bloom Lake Erie has experienced in decades

**An osprey**

## Vocabulary

**natural resource**
useful thing found in nature (e.g., lake, forest)

**dump**
to put down or drop something in a careless way

**dilute**
to make weaker by adding water

**suffer**
to be damaged or experience a loss or injury

**damage**
harm or injury

**foul**
extremely unpleasant

**condition**
the particular state that something or someone is in

**treatment**
a process to protect, preserve, or clean something

# Reading Skills Comprehension Practice

 **Part 1** Explain how the different kinds of typeface found in this passage can help the reader.

_____

_____

_____

_____

## Lake Erie's Struggle to Survive

### POLLUTING LAKE ERIE

### SAVING LAKE ERIE

 **Part 2** Explain what you learned about Lake Erie by looking at the different kinds of typeface on the page.

_____

_____

_____

_____

**Part 3** Typeface can give the reader a clue about the main idea of a text. Write the main idea of this text below.

_____

_____

_____

# Comprehension Review

**Fill in the best answer for each question.**

_____ **① The typeface tells you that this passage is _mostly_ about _____**

Ⓐ Lake Erie.

Ⓑ maps.

Ⓒ the Great Lakes.

Ⓓ an osprey.

_____ **② Why is the title in large typeface?**

Ⓐ It is the least important thing.

Ⓑ It comes first.

Ⓒ It tells the topic of the passage.

Ⓓ It is the name of a place.

_____ **③ The typefaces help readers to _____**

Ⓐ learn more about lakes.

Ⓑ learn how the Great Lakes formed.

Ⓒ find out how Lake Erie's problems were solved.

Ⓓ understand the important ideas.

_____ **④ What is an _ecosystem_?**

Ⓐ a system that exists in lakes and oceans

Ⓑ a complex group of organisms and their environment

Ⓒ an ecological group

Ⓓ an explanation of how plants and animals work together

_____ **⑤ _Recently, scientists were alarmed to discover a "dead zone" in the lake._ What is a _dead zone_?**

Ⓐ an area where only dead animals are found

Ⓑ an area with no algae

Ⓒ an area with low levels of oxygen and no living things except algae

Ⓓ an area with few living things

_____ **⑥ Which topic would probably come _next_?**

Ⓐ Wonders of the World

Ⓑ Lakes of the Northwest

Ⓒ A Look at the Great Lakes

Ⓓ The Future of Lake Erie

# Word Power

**Choose the English word from the Vocabulary list that correctly matches the definition.**

 to make weaker by adding water

_____

 useful thing found in nature (e.g., lake, forest)

_____

 extremely unpleasant

_____

 to put down or drop something in a careless way

_____

**Reflecting on your reading** means thinking about your personal responses to a text as well as your opinions about it.

Florence Nightingale inspects a hospital ward during the Crimean War.

Florence Nightingale

# Florence Nightingale

## Skill Overview

Readers reflect on text when they think about what has been read and form ideas about it. Reflecting helps readers make sense of what they read and connect it with what is already known.

16

In 1854, a nurse named Florence Nightingale was determined to make a difference during the Crimean War. Nightingale organized a group of nurses to care for **wounded** British soldiers. She and the other nurses boarded a ship in England and set sail for a hospital in Scutari, Turkey. When they arrived at the hospital, the nurses saw that it was surrounded by mud and trash. However, the worst was yet to come.

Upon entering the hospital, Nightingale and her fellow nurses could not believe the **deplorable** conditions these soldiers had to **endure**. Everything in the hospital was dirty and falling apart. Rats moved about freely. Soldiers who were sick or injured lay on bed after bed. But there were not enough beds to go around, so many other soldiers were on the floor. The hospital had few **supplies**. The soldiers often went without food and medicine. There were not enough clothes, blankets, or equipment.

The hospital's doctors and staff did not welcome the nurses. They felt that the nurses would be more trouble than they were worth. They would not even allow the nurses to help the soldiers. The nurses were not given any supplies except for a daily pint of water intended for drinking and washing.

Every day, more sick and wounded soldiers arrived at the hospital from the battlefield. Conditions got increasingly worse, and the situation seemed hopeless. But Nightingale was more determined than ever to make the hospital a better place. Against army **regulations**, she went to Constantinople to purchase supplies. She made sure the orderlies cleaned and scrubbed everything in the hospital. She had the patients' clothes washed regularly. She managed to obtain money that was raised in England to buy additional supplies. Not only did Nightingale attend to all these administrative duties, but she also spent countless hours caring for the sick and dying. The doctors were inspired by her **dedication**, and the soldiers felt that she was an angel of mercy. Nightingale ensured the survival of many soldiers who might otherwise have died.

In 1856, after the war ended, Nightingale went home to England. She was honored as a hero for her work in the Crimean War. Once home, Nightingale's **commitment** to helping others continued. She worked to improve the quality of army and **civilian** hospitals. She is known today as the founder of modern nursing.

## Vocabulary

**wounded**
injured, especially with a cut or hole in the skin

✿**deplorable**
very bad; horrible

**endure**
to suffer something difficult, unpleasant, or painful

**supplies**
food or other things necessary for living

**regulation**
an official rule

**dedication**
strong support for or loyalty to something or someone

**commitment**
a willingness to give your time and energy to something that you believe in

**civilian**
something that is nonmilitary

**Nightingale receiving the wounded at Scutari**

# Reading Skills Comprehension Practice

Write your ideas or opinions about the passage after reading it.

I think Nightingale was very courageous because she devoted herself to the front line to take care of those wounded soldiers.

_____

_____

_____

## Part 2

Write about how this passage relates to your life.

This passage relates to my life because I've been to the hospital countless times. I can imagine what it is like in the hospital.

_____

_____

_____

Suggest additional information that could have been added to this passage.

I think more information about the soldiers' reaction and gratefulness toward Nightingale could have been added.

_____

_____

_____

# Comprehension Review

**Fill in the best answer for each question.**

_____ ❶ **Which of these would help you picture the hospital where Florence Nightingale worked?**

Ⓐ finding a picture of Florence Nightingale

Ⓑ thinking about hospitals you have visited

Ⓒ drawing a picture of a ship

Ⓓ reading about soldiers

_____ ❷ **What would have happened if the hospital had been left the way it was?**

Ⓐ Florence Nightingale would still be a hero.

Ⓑ The soldiers would have gotten well more quickly.

Ⓒ Many more soldiers would have died.

Ⓓ The doctors and staff would have cleaned up the hospital.

_____ ❸ **How do today's hospitals differ from the hospital in Scutari?**

Ⓐ Today's hospitals are much cleaner and safer.

Ⓑ Today's hospitals have doctors.

Ⓒ Today's hospitals are much dirtier and more unsafe.

Ⓓ Today's hospitals do not provide food and medicine.

_____ ❹ *Upon entering the hospital, Nightingale and her nurses could not believe the deplorable conditions these soldiers had to endure.*

**What does _deplorable_ mean in this sentence?**

Ⓐ friendly

Ⓑ watery

Ⓒ terrible

Ⓓ rich

_____ ❺ **Florence Nightingale was probably from _____**

Ⓐ the United States.

Ⓑ England.

Ⓒ Turkey.

Ⓓ Russia.

_____ ❻ **The soldiers were _____ Florence Nightingale.**

Ⓐ grateful to

Ⓑ afraid of

Ⓒ angry with

Ⓓ jealous of

# Word Power

**Choose the English word from the Vocabulary list that correctly matches the definition.**

 something that is nonmilitary

_____

 very bad; horrible

_____

 an official rule

_____

 food or other things necessary for living

_____

## An Unexpected Sound

### Skill Overview

**Use of language** refers to the specific words that an author uses to help readers acquire meaning from a text. Examples include **vivid verbs**, **strong adjectives**, **similes**, **metaphors**, and **dialogue**.

17

When they entered the **subway** station, they entered a whole different world. Initially, it was the **odor** that caused the two small boys to crinkle their noses. As they walked through the station, the boys touched the metal railings, but the mother **reprimanded** them, "Don't touch anything!" She grabbed a tissue from her pocket and immediately cleaned both boys' fingers.

The screeching of wheels and the thundering sound that came from the dark tunnel were deafening. The mother held the boys' wrists so firmly that their fingers turned a bright plum color.

At first glance, there didn't appear to be many people waiting for the subway, but when the doors opened, the stampede began. **Impatient** shoving and turn-taking ensued as people trampled in and out, rushing to beat the slamming of the doors. The mother hoisted a boy on each hip and quickly pushed through the doors.

With every other seat taken, the mother had no choice but to grip a metal pole. The frazzled expression on her face made an older man get up and offer his seat to her. The mother immediately sat, holding her boys close. When the doors opened, the subway poured out a stream of people. The mother looked frantically for an exit. With each little boy's hand tightly in hers, the mother wove through the **crowd**.

Amidst the loud hum of voices, a **distinct** sound sliced through. The younger son's pale-blue gaze followed the source of the **unexpected** music. With people all around him, the boy could get only a glimpse of the violinist by the token machines. His black hair was dark like a starless night sky, his face bent down toward his instrument.

"Let's stop and listen," he called loudly to his mother.

The boys **dragged** their feet and leaned in the direction of the violinist. The bright, hopeful music rose from the crowd and cut through the dull pounding of people's footsteps.

"Just for a minute?" they asked their mother. "Can we listen for just a minute?"

The mother's quick mechanical steps halted, and she spun around to scold them. But the music made her suddenly stop. As she stood among a flurry of strangers, she tilted her head to the side and heard the music for the first time since they had left the subway car. For a few long moments, the boys and mother remembered the days before moving to the city, when they had called another place home. She gave the boys her first smile of the morning, and they walked toward the exit, no longer in a hurry.

## Vocabulary

**subway**
a railway system in which electric trains travel along passages below ground

**odor**
a smell, often one that is unpleasant

✿**reprimand**
to say that something was done incorrectly; to scold

✿**impatient**
unwilling to wait; wanting something immediately

**crowd**
a large group of people who have come together

**distinct**
clearly noticeable

✿**unexpected**
surprising because it was not expected

**drag**
to move something by pulling it along a surface

# Reading Skills Comprehension Practice

**Part 1** Describe what you noticed about the use of language when you first read this passage.

When I first listened to and read the passage, I noticed
_____
_____
_____

**Part 2** Describe the tone of this passage.

The tone of this passage is
_____

**Part 3** List three examples of descriptive language in the passage.

1. His black hair was dark like a starless night sky.
_____

2. _____
_____

3. _____
_____

4. _____
_____

# Comprehension Review

**Fill in the best answer for each question.**

**❶ Which of these is a simile?**

Ⓐ Impatient shoving and turn-taking ensued as people trampled in and out.

Ⓑ The mother's quick, mechanical steps halted.

Ⓒ His black hair was dark like a starless night sky.

Ⓓ The bright, hopeful music rose from the crowd.

**❷ *Amidst the loud hum of voices, a distinct sound sliced through.***

**Here, *sound sliced* is an example of** _____

Ⓐ a metaphor.

Ⓑ point of view.

Ⓒ a simile.

Ⓓ personification.

**❸ *... but when the doors opened, the stampede began.***

**What is the author comparing the subway riders to?**

Ⓐ a garden    Ⓑ fish

Ⓒ snakes      Ⓓ cattle

**❹ What is the overall mood in the subway station?**

Ⓐ bright and hopeful

Ⓑ ominous and fearful

Ⓒ hurried and busy

Ⓓ exciting and vibrant

**❺ What in the subway station caught the younger son's attention?**

Ⓐ music from a violin

Ⓑ the stampede of people

Ⓒ his frantic mother

Ⓓ the metal railings

**❻ What can you infer about the mother?**

Ⓐ She doesn't care for music.

Ⓑ She enjoys the lively buzz of the subway station.

Ⓒ She wishes her sons were better behaved.

Ⓓ She misses living outside of the city.

# Word Power

**Choose the English word from the Vocabulary list that correctly matches the definition.**

 **1** to say that something was done incorrectly; to scold

_____

 **2** unwilling to wait; wanting something immediately

_____

 **3** surprising because it was not expected

_____

 **4** a large group of people who have come together

_____

Burning fossil fuels pollutes the air.

Solar panels on rooftops help generate electricity.

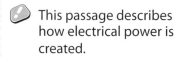
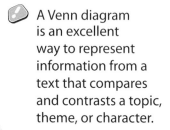
# New Ways to Make Electricity

## Skill Overview

Authors use a compare-and-contrast structure to show similarities and differences between topics, events, or people. Readers may recognize this pattern by noticing certain signal words, such as *like*, *but*, *also*, and *no*.

 18

Think of how you used electricity today. Did you cook breakfast in the microwave, turn on a light, or use a computer? All of these things use electrical power, and electrical power must be created. Usually this means that a power plant burns gas, oil, or coal to **generate electricity**. But these are all fossil fuels, and just like fossils, these fuels formed deep underground over millions of years. Dead plants and animals rotted, and after millions of years and lots of pressure from the weight of the ground above, they changed into gas, oil, or coal. The world has used fossil fuels for energy for more than 100 years. However, burning them causes significant **pollution**, and Earth is

Solar electric cars are cleaner for the environment.

Wind power is a clean way to produce electricity.

quickly being depleted of fossil fuels. Within 40 years, there probably won't be any left—and we certainly can't wait a million years for more to be generated.

Scientists are trying to figure out the solution to the potential problem of **resource depletion**. They are looking for new ways to make electricity, and they would prefer to find new ways that don't cause pollution. Their hope is to find renewable energy sources, which means that, unlike fossil fuels, they can be replaced by nature. What can possibly meet those demands? The Sun and the wind can.

Right now, no one knows the **optimal** way to capture the Sun's rays and turn them into electrical power. Many homes and businesses are using **solar** panels to generate some of the electricity they need. Japan and other countries have constructed some houses with solar roof **tiles**. These tiles collect sunshine even on overcast days. So far, the tiles have worked so well that they can make all of the electricity a family needs each day. Some cars that use solar tiles for part of their power have already been built.

For hundreds of years, people in the Netherlands used windmills for their energy. Today's windmills are taller and have lightweight blades to catch more wind. Some have propellers mounted on heads that can turn; this lets the windmill get the most wind possible, no matter which way the wind blows. In the driest parts of the western United States, wind farms have sprung up. Hundreds of windmills stand on otherwise unused land. The electricity they generate powers homes and businesses in cities many miles away.

## Vocabulary

**generate**
to make or create something

**electricity**
a form of energy, produced in several ways, to power lights, generate heat, run appliances, etc.

**pollution**
damage caused to water, air, etc., by harmful substances or waste

**resource**
a useful or valuable possession or quality of a country, organization, or person

**depletion**
the process of emptying or using up

**optimal**
the most ideal

**solar**
of or from the Sun

**tile**
a thin, usually square or rectangular piece of baked clay or plastic used for covering roofs, floors, walls, etc.

# Reading Skills Comprehension Practice

**Part 1**  Tell how the author uses a compare-and-contrast pattern in the passage.

_____

_____

_____

**Part 2**  Fill in the Venn diagram below by comparing and contrasting two different ways of making electricity.

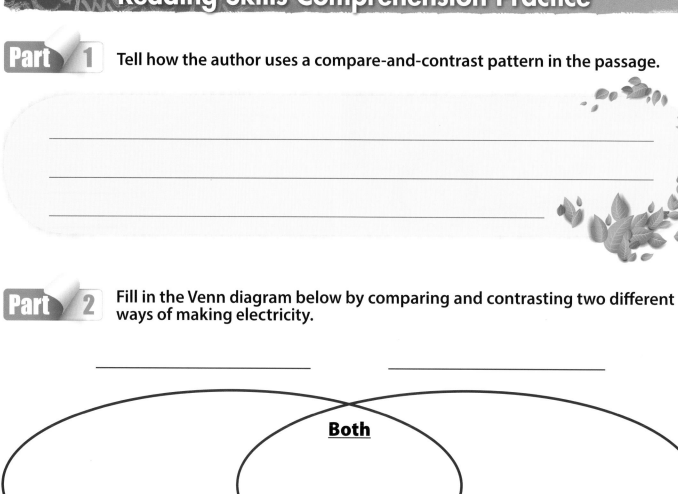

**Both**

**Part 3**  Fill in the Venn diagram to compare and contrast fossil fuels and renewable energy sources.

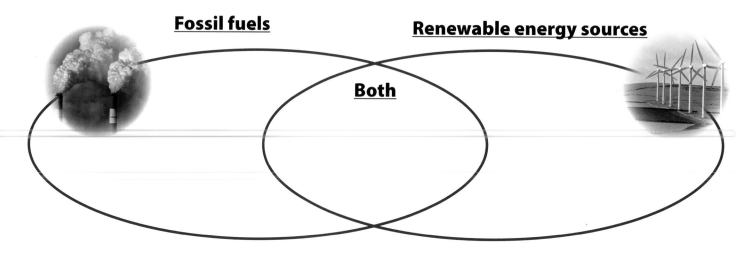

**Fossil fuels**

**Renewable energy sources**

**Both**

# Comprehension Review

**Fill in the best answer for each question.**

_____ ❶ How are renewable energy sources unlike fossil fuels?

Ⓐ They never run out.
Ⓑ They are used only in Japan.
Ⓒ They cause more pollution.
Ⓓ They rely on humans to produce energy.

_____ ❷ How do fossil fuels primarily differ from renewable energy sources?

Ⓐ Fossil fuels come from the Earth.
Ⓑ Fossil fuels never run out.
Ⓒ Fossil fuels pollute the air.
Ⓓ Fossil fuels are more efficient.

_____ ❸ How are today's windmills different from those used in the Netherlands in years past?

Ⓐ They are shorter.
Ⓑ They are taller.
Ⓒ They have more blades.
Ⓓ They catch less wind.

_____ ❹ What two forms of renewable energy are discussed in the passage?

Ⓐ wind and water
Ⓑ solar and water
Ⓒ biomass
Ⓓ solar and wind

_____ ❺ How long has the world used fossil fuels for energy?

Ⓐ over 100 years
Ⓑ 40 years
Ⓒ over 1,000 years
Ⓓ millions of years

_____ ❻ What is the purpose of this passage?

Ⓐ to get readers to visit Japan and the Netherlands
Ⓑ to tell about new ways to make electricity
Ⓒ to give instructions for putting solar panels on a roof
Ⓓ to tell how fossil fuels are used

# Word Power

**Choose the English word from the Vocabulary list that correctly matches the definition.**

the process of emptying or using up

_____

the most ideal

_____

to make or create something

_____

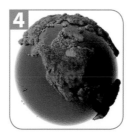
a useful or valuable possession or quality of a country, organization, or person

_____

# Ecosystem Energy Exchange

## Skill Overview

A reader's prior knowledge includes information obtained from other texts as well as from personal experiences. When readers are able to make connections between their prior knowledge and what they read, reading comprehension is enhanced.

An ecosystem is made up of many different **organisms**. Some of the organisms are **autotrophs**, or producers, that make their own food. The rest are **heterotrophs**, or consumers, that eat other organisms for food. The way that all the organisms **interact** helps us understand how the ecosystem works.

## Food Chains and Webs

A food chain is a list of organisms that eat each other. A cricket might eat grass. A lizard eats the cricket. A hawk eats the lizard. The grass, the cricket, the lizard, and the hawk make a food chain. This is an easy way to see how different organisms are connected within an ecosystem.

However, most animals eat more than one kind of food. Then those animals are often eaten by more than one kind of **predator**. A food chain doesn't really tell us the whole story— it's too simplistic.

Imagine you drew all the plants and animals in an area. Then imagine drawing lines from each one to all the organisms it eats or is eaten by. You would have a very **complicated** web of lines. These networks of lines are food webs.

**As part of a food chain, this lizard eats a cricket.**

**As part of a food chain, an eagle eats a lizard.**

# Energy Pyramid

An energy pyramid shows the **exchange** of energy among organisms in an ecosystem. Organisms get energy from other organisms by eating them.

The bottom of the pyramid is composed of producers. They are usually plants that **provide** food for primary consumers, such as zebras and gazelles. The primary consumers, in turn, provide food for secondary consumers, such as lions. As the pyramid narrows to the top, the number of consumers decreases.

Energy levels also decrease as you move up the pyramid. Every time something gets eaten, energy is lost. There is enough energy for only a few animals at the top.

When looking at an energy pyramid, keep in mind that it doesn't tell the whole story the way a food web does. Many more plants and animals are involved in the exchange of energy in an ecosystem than the plants and animals shown in the pyramid.

## Vocabulary

**organism**
a living thing

✪**autotroph**
an organism that produces its own food

✪**heterotroph**
an organism that eats other organisms for food

**interact**
to communicate with or react to

✪**predator**
an animal that hunts, kills, and eats other animals

**complicated**
involving a lot of different parts in a way that is difficult to understand

**exchange**
the act of giving something to someone and them giving you something else

**provide**
to supply or make available

This energy pyramid shows the exchange of energy from one source to another.

INCREASED SIZE

DECREASED ENERGY

INCREASED SIZE

DECREASED ENERGY

# Reading Skills Comprehension Practice

**Part 1**  Describe a time when you read or learned something that helped you extend or adjust your existing knowledge about a topic.

_____

_____

_____

**Part 2**  Brainstorm what you already know about this topic. Record your ideas in the chart.

**1.** to supply or make available

**2.** _____

**3.** _____

**Ecosystem Energy Exchange**

**4.** _____

**5.** _____

**6.** _____

**Part 3**  Now that you have read the entire passage, tell how your knowledge of this topic has changed.

_I learned that_ _____

_____

_____

# Comprehension Review

**Fill in the best answer for each question.**

_____ **①** Knowing what a food chain is helps you to understand what a _____ is.

ⓐ food choice

ⓑ cricket

ⓒ food web

ⓓ hawk

_____ **②** One thing this passage tells you about food chains is that _____

ⓐ food chains give the most information about how an ecosystem works.

ⓑ some animals eat grass.

ⓒ animals eat other animals.

ⓓ they are too simple to explain how an ecosystem works.

_____ **③** What does this passage tell you about autotrophs and heterotrophs?

ⓐ Autotrophs make their own food, and heterotrophs eat other organisms.

ⓑ Heterotrophs are not part of a food chain, but autotrophs are.

ⓒ Both autotrophs and heterotrophs eat other organisms.

ⓓ Both kinds of organisms make their own food.

_____ **④** Which of these gives the *most* information about the organisms in an ecosystem?

ⓐ food pyramid

ⓑ food chain

ⓒ food web

ⓓ autotroph

_____ **⑤** Why does energy decrease as you move up a food pyramid?

ⓐ Eating something takes very little energy.

ⓑ Every time something gets eaten, energy is lost.

ⓒ There is only enough energy for a few animals at the top.

ⓓ The bottom of the pyramid is made up of consumers.

_____ **⑥** A zebra is an example of a(n) _____

ⓐ food web.

ⓑ autotroph.

ⓒ primary producer.

ⓓ primary consumer.

# Word Power

**Choose the English word from the Vocabulary list that correctly matches the definition.**

 an organism that eats other organisms for food

_____

 an organism that produces its own food

_____

 a living thing

_____

 the act of giving something to someone and them giving you something else

_____

# The Viking Ships

## Skill Overview

A topic sentence introduces and summarizes the information in a text. It is usually the first or last sentence in a paragraph. Effective readers use topic sentences to determine the main idea and better understand the text.

🎧 20

The Vikings were a group of people whose sailors **explored** the North Atlantic Ocean from 700 to 1100 A.D. They lived in the countries now known as Denmark, Norway, and Sweden. Because they lived so close to the sea, they used water as their primary means of travel.

**Vocabulary**

**explore**
to search and discover

⚙**keel**
a long, narrow piece of
wood mounted under a
ship

**steer**
to control the direction of
a vehicle

**route**
a path from one place to
another

**settlement**
a place where people
come to live or the
process of settling in such
a place

**descendant**
a person who is related to
others and who lives after
them, such as their child
or grandchild

**inhabit**
to live in a place

⚙**endow**
to provide with something

Over the years, the Vikings became expert shipbuilders. They even developed a new way to build ships that allowed them to travel farther by sea than was possible before. Their ships were the first to have a **keel**—a long, narrow piece of wood attached to the bottom of the ship that helped to **steer** it. Even better, it kept the ship from rolling with each wave, allowing it to move faster. Because the ship could get to places more rapidly, it could go much farther without stopping for new supplies of food and water.

The front of a Viking ship curved up into a wooden carving of a dragon's head. This carving helped people identify a Viking ship while it was still far away.

A wooden
carving of a
dragon's head
on a Viking ship

Out in the ocean, the ships needed the wind to blow their huge wool sail, but on a river, people rowed the ship. Each ship had 15 to 30 pairs of oars. If the ship was narrow, one man would work two oars; in wider ships, one man worked each oar.

The ships allowed the Vikings to establish trade **routes** throughout Europe. The Vikings actually discovered North America about 500 years before Columbus did, and they even set up a small **settlement** in what is now Canada, but it lasted only a few years. Viking ships carried settlers to Greenland and Iceland. Greenland is actually a very icy country, but they called it *Greenland* to get people to go there. The **descendants** of the Vikings still **inhabit** both of these countries.

All Vikings were proud of their ships; in fact, when they died, many rich Viking men and women were buried in a ship. Included in the ship were the dead person's belongings, such as jewelry and weapons. The Vikings believed that the ships would **endow** these people with a safe journey to the land of the dead.

# Reading Skills Comprehension Practice

 Write a topic sentence that is appropriate for one of the paragraphs in this passage.

**Topic Sentence** _____

 **Part 2** Write the main idea of the passage, which incorporates the topic sentence you wrote in Part 1.

**Main Idea** _____

 **Part 3** In the graphic organizer below, record some of the details the author uses to support the main idea of this passage.

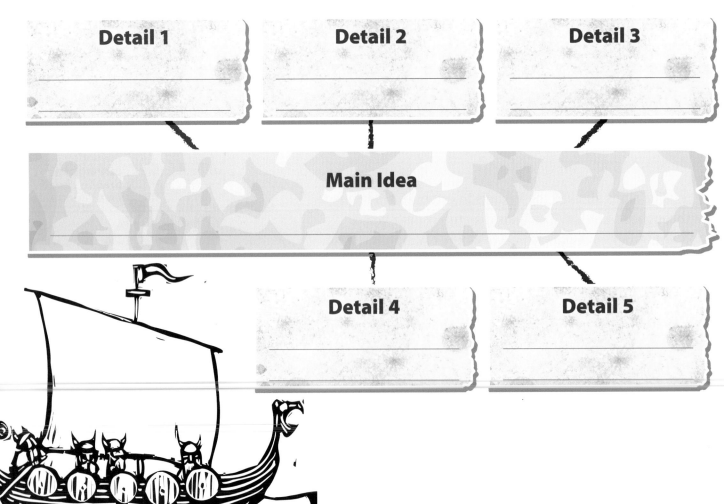

| Detail 1 | Detail 2 | Detail 3 |
| --- | --- | --- |
| | | |

**Main Idea**

| Detail 4 | Detail 5 |
| --- | --- |
| | |

# Comprehension Review

**Fill in the best answer for each question.**

_____ **1** *The ships allowed the Vikings to establish trade routes throughout Europe.*

**This sentence tells you that the main idea in this passage is _____**

Ⓐ where the Vikings lived.

Ⓑ how ships were an important part of their livelihood.

Ⓒ what the Vikings' beliefs were.

Ⓓ how ships were built.

_____ **2** *Over the years, they became expert shipbuilders.*

**Which detail *best* supports this sentence?**

Ⓐ Each ship had oars.

Ⓑ Vikings were proud of their ships.

Ⓒ They developed a new way to build ships that allowed them to travel farther.

Ⓓ Rich Viking men and women were buried in ships.

_____ **3** **Which of these is the most important sentence for the third paragraph?**

Ⓐ The front of a Viking ship curved up into a wooden carving of a dragon's head.

Ⓑ Out in the ocean, ships needed the wind to blow their huge wool sail.

Ⓒ Over the years, the Vikings became expert shipbuilders.

Ⓓ Each ship had oars.

_____ **4** **Which is the *least* important point about Viking ships?**

Ⓐ They were the first to have a keel.

Ⓑ The wooden carving on the front helped people identify each ship.

Ⓒ Vikings were proud of their ships.

Ⓓ They let the Vikings establish trade routes throughout Europe.

_____ **5** **What is the purpose of this passage?**

Ⓐ to explain how to build a ship

Ⓑ to tell about the Vikings and their ships

Ⓒ to get readers to travel to Greenland

Ⓓ to describe how Vikings looked

_____ **6** **Which statement about the Vikings is true?**

Ⓐ They discovered North America about 500 years before Columbus.

Ⓑ They explored the North Atlantic from 700 to 1200 a.d.

Ⓒ They carried settlers from Greenland to Norway.

Ⓓ They lived in Denmark, Norway, and Iceland.

# Word Power

**Choose the English word from the Vocabulary list that correctly matches the definition.**

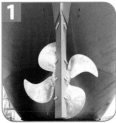
**1** a long, narrow piece of wood mounted under a ship

_____

**2** to provide with something

_____

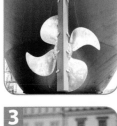
**3** to search and discover

_____

**4** a path from one place to another

_____

# Slater Copy Machines, Inc.

## Skill Overview

An author writes a text with a purpose in mind—often to persuade, inform, or entertain. Authors use specific devices to express the purpose. When readers are familiar with tools such as **word choice**, **persuasive techniques**, and **language structure**, they can more quickly determine the author's message.

### Reading Tip

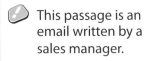 This passage is an email written by a sales manager.

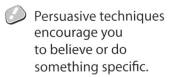 Persuasive techniques encourage you to believe or do something specific.

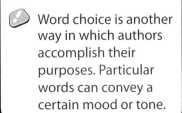 Word choice is another way in which authors accomplish their purposes. Particular words can convey a certain mood or tone.

## Memo

**To:** Sales Force
**From:** Carter Billings, Sales Manager
**Re:** Sales **Figures** and Goals

Congratulations! You have done a great job selling this **quarter** (April to June). The total **revenue** you brought in this quarter was $1,660,000. Our total revenue is up 13% from the previous quarter. We also sold 2,219 more units. But before you celebrate, consider this: Much of this **increase** is because of major new accounts that Steve and Alicia brought in. When we factor in the sales brought in by everyone else, the numbers are far less **impressive**. Total sales from all others combined are up only 3% from last quarter. Each of you must open new accounts over the next quarter, or those total sales figures will likely fall.

## Goals

I know it's tough out there, but we must do better. Our goal is to increase revenues by at least 2% over this quarter's revenues. To do that, every salesperson will have to work hard. You must hang on to old accounts and bring in new ones. I know you can do it. So go out there and sell! By the way, Alicia is in the lead for the sales bonus this **fiscal** year. Unless someone **overtakes** her in the next three months, she wins the Caribbean vacation!

There are 5,000,000 copy machines in Europe, purchased by 100,000 businesses. We have targeted 25,000 businesses in Eastern Europe that use copiers. There are 30,000 businesses using copiers in Western Europe. There are 45,000 in northern Europe. We must go after these businesses. Also, the Statistics Department predicts the number of businesses needing copiers will increase by 10% over next five years. This creates increased **opportunities** for us.

**figure**
the symbol for a number or an amount expressed in numbers

**quarter**
one of four equal or almost equal parts of something

**revenue**
money that a company makes

**increase**
to become larger in amount or size

**impressive**
drawing admiration and attention

✪**fiscal**
relating to money and finances

**overtake**
to go past something in amount or degree

**opportunity**
the possibility of doing something

# Reading Skills Comprehension Practice

 **Part 1** Tell what you think the sales manager's purpose is for writing the email.

The sales manager's purpose for writing this email is

_____

_____

_____

 **Part 2** Tell how the sales manager in the passage uses persuasive techniques to help accomplish his purpose for writing this text.

| Example of Persuasive Technique | How It Helps Accomplish the Purpose |
| --- | --- |
| | |

 **Part 3** Tell how the sales manager's word choices help accomplish his or her purpose for writing this text.

| Example of Word Choice | How It Helps Accomplish the Purpose |
| --- | --- |
| | |

# Comprehension Review

**Fill in the best answer for each question.**

**❶** _I know it's tough out there, but we must do better._

The sales manager uses the word must to tell you _____

Ⓐ about new copiers.

Ⓑ that there is a new law.

Ⓒ how important it is to make sales.

Ⓓ that copier sales do not matter.

**❷ Which phrase tells you that the sales manager has both good news and bad news?**

Ⓐ Congratulations!

Ⓑ We also sold 2,219 more units.

Ⓒ The total revenue you brought in this quarter was $1,660,000.

Ⓓ But before you celebrate, consider this:

**❸ Which sentence will best motivate the sales force to sell more?**

Ⓐ Congratulations!

Ⓑ There are 5,000,000 copy machines in Europe, purchased by 100,000 businesses.

Ⓒ I know you can do it.

Ⓓ We also sold 2,219 more units.

**❹ What does the sales manager want the sales force to do?**

Ⓐ get more training

Ⓑ take a vacation

Ⓒ learn how to repair copiers

Ⓓ sell more copiers

**❺ You can infer that _____**

Ⓐ this was the worst sales quarter the company has had.

Ⓑ Alicia is a good salesperson.

Ⓒ this company only sells in the East.

Ⓓ the number of businesses needing copiers will fall.

**❻** _Our total revenue is up 13% from the previous quarter._

What is another word for _revenue_?

Ⓐ copiers

Ⓑ sales

Ⓒ companies

Ⓓ bonuses

# Word Power

**Choose the English word from the Vocabulary list that correctly matches the definition.**

 relating to money and finances

_____

 drawing admiration and attention

_____

 money that a company makes

_____

 to become larger in amount or size

_____

# LESSON 22
## Author's Point of View

### Reading Tip

As you listen to and read the passage, try to find clues about the point of view the author uses in the passage.

# LUCKY ME

## Skill Overview

**Point of view** refers to the specific perspective that a piece of literature expresses to its audience. Usually the point of view is assigned to the narrator, with the story told in first-person or third-person point of view.

🎧 22

I always do homework at the kitchen counter. The warm hum of the dishwasher drowns out the noise in my head so that I can **concentrate**. But tonight, I stare at my paper—empty, endless, and **blank**, just like my ideas. Our assignment in language arts is to prepare for writing about why we are lucky, and all day I have been **bothered** by this because I do not feel lucky. I've never felt lucky, and I can't think of anything that makes me lucky. I feel like a person in an assembly line who

plods along without anything exciting happening.

Oh, I could write about how my friends are lucky. Miguel is lucky because his brother drives him to and from school in a red Mustang. He revs up the engine like he's about to take off in the Indy 500 before spinning out of the school parking lot. And Abby visits her father on weekends and always comes to school on Monday with some sort of trinket that everyone wants.

I go into the living room, where a glamorous game-show wannabe in her sequins, and **baubles**, and plastic smile gestures as each Powerball™ number flies to its final destination. No winners, and therefore, no luck for anyone. No winners and therefore, no luck. Suddenly, a powerful drumroll introduces the nightly news. Top stories reveal bad luck: A powerful storm forces thousands to **evacuate**, a multicar accident closes the interstate, and contaminated drinking water threatens the lives of refugees in a third-world country. Bad luck everywhere.

While walking to school the next morning, I notice a sign for a lost cat. I stop to admire the picture. A pair of yellow eyes lights up the furry, gray face. Some kid's probably bawling, waiting for the cat's return.

A couple blocks down, another sign states "Moving Sale." I can't imagine living anywhere but here. I'd have to make new friends and leave my neighborhood, the arcade down the block, and the best pepperoni pizza in the country.

At school, I am **surrounded** by friends in the cafeteria. I crunch an apple from my family's apple-picking **expedition** last weekend, and the sweet juice dribbles down my chin. Laughter hugs me tightly. An upcoming dance inspires my friends. Our win over our crosstown rival **empowers** them. My only concern is the science test next period.

Now I look forward to language arts because I have plenty of ideas. How lucky is that?

## Vocabulary

**concentrate**
to direct your attention or your efforts toward a particular activity, subject, or problem

**blank**
empty or clear, or containing no information or mark

**bother**
to annoy or cause problems for someone

✪**bauble**
trinket

**evacuate**
to move a large number of people from a dangerous place to a safe place

**surround**
to be all around something

**expedition**
an organized trip

✪**empower**
to give someone official authority or the freedom to do something

89

# Reading Skills Comprehension Practice

A **first-person** story is narrated by one character who uses words such as *I*, *me*, and *we*.

A **third-person** story is told by a narrator who is separate from the characters of the story and uses words such as *he*, *she*, and *they*.

**Part 1** Use the passage to answer the questions below.

**1.** Why do you think the author chose this point of view?

_____

**2.** Did it make the story more interesting? Why or why not?

_____

**Part 2** Rewrite a sentence from the passage using third-person point of view.

| Original Sentence | At school, I am surrounded by friends in the cafeteria. |

| Rewrite | At school, Kat is surrounded by friends in the cafeteria. |

| Original Sentence | _____ |

| Rewrite | _____ |

**Part 3** List the words that indicate this passage is written in first-person point of view.

| I | | | |

# Comprehension Review

**Fill in the best answer for each question.**

_____ **1** This story is told from _____ point of view.
- Ⓐ the narrator's
- Ⓑ Miguel's
- Ⓒ Miguel's brother's
- Ⓓ Abby's

_____ **2** What is the narrator's point of view about luck at the beginning of the story?
- Ⓐ The narrator is happy to write about luck.
- Ⓑ The narrator does not believe luck is possible.
- Ⓒ The narrator does not feel lucky.
- Ⓓ The narrator feels extremely lucky.

_____ **3** What changes the narrator's point of view about luck?
- Ⓐ a lottery ticket
- Ⓑ remembering the good things in life
- Ⓒ a red Mustang
- Ⓓ Abby's visit to her father

_____ **4** *Laughter hugs me tightly.*
**What is this an example of?**
- Ⓐ alliteration
- Ⓑ metaphor
- Ⓒ simile
- Ⓓ personification

_____ **5** What is the main idea of this passage?
- Ⓐ The good things in life make us lucky.
- Ⓑ Winning the Powerball™ lottery is easy.
- Ⓒ There are several steps to writing a language arts paper.
- Ⓓ It is a good idea to post signs if you lose a pet.

_____ **6** Which of these is a good prediction?
- Ⓐ The author will not be able to write the language arts paper.
- Ⓑ The author will find it easy to write the language arts paper.
- Ⓒ The author will buy a winning lottery ticket.
- Ⓓ The author will feel very unlucky.

# Word Power

**Choose the English word from the Vocabulary list that correctly matches the definition.**

**1** to move a large number of people from a dangerous place to a safe place
_____

**2** an organized trip
_____

**3** empty or clear, or containing no information or mark
_____

**4** trinket
_____

The skeletal system

# SYSTEMS FOR MOVEMENT

## Skill Overview

Drawing conclusions involves analyzing information and comparing it to one's own background knowledge. Authors often omit certain information because they rely on readers to consider their prior knowledge as they read.

More than six billion humans live on earth. We look different, act differently, and think different thoughts. However, we all share the same basic **structure**, and our bodies all have the same kinds of **systems** inside. This is because we are all human.

All living things have **genes**, and humans all have human genes. Genes help **determine** how a person looks and behaves. Many **traits** are **inherited**, such as body size, eye color, and hair texture. So are chances for developing certain diseases and even personality traits. However, everyone inherits the body's most important systems.

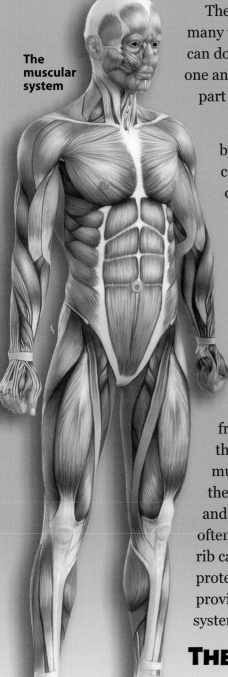

The muscular system

The human body is like a machine with many working parts. Together, these parts can do a lot of work. The parts depend on one another to **support** the machine. Each part has specific needs and abilities.

Scientists **categorize** body parts by the work they do. Just as every community has people who perform different jobs, the body has different parts that do different jobs.

A community needs all its workers to do their jobs, or there will be trouble. The body needs all its parts to work well, too. If they don't, there will be trouble, usually in the form of illness or injury.

## THE SKELETAL SYSTEM

The skeletal system is the framework for the body. It supports the body, gives it shape, and supports muscles that allow the body to move. All the bones in the body are linked by joints, and together they form the skeleton. Bones often protect vital organs. For example, the rib cage protects the heart, and the skull protects the brain. The skeletal system also provides substances that aid the immune system.

## THE MUSCULAR SYSTEM

The skeleton could not work without the muscular system, which performs all body movements. Some muscles attach to bones, whereas others work on their own. Muscles can contract, or get shorter, creating a pulling force. Most muscles come in pairs so that one muscle pulls your body one way and the other muscle pulls your body the other way. This allows you to move.

There are three types of muscles: skeletal, cardiac, and smooth. Skeletal muscles are used for activities such as running, lifting, and swimming, and these muscles tire easily. In contrast, cardiac muscle is found in the wall of the heart, where it contracts tirelessly to create your heartbeat. Lastly, smooth muscles perform vital functions such as swallowing.

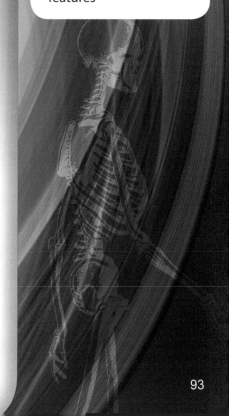

**Part 1**
Tell what conclusions you can draw about this passage from the title alone.

Based on the title of this passage, I can conclude that

_____

_____

**Part 2**
In the chart below, record the explicit and implicit information that helped you draw conclusions while reading this passage.

### Explicit Information

**1.** Genes help determine how a person

will look and behave.

**2.** _____

_____

**3.** _____

_____

### Implicit Information

**1.** Each system of the body depends

on the others.

**2.** _____

_____

**3.** _____

_____

**Part 3**
Describe any personal connections that you have to the topic in this passage. What knowledge or experience do you have that relates to this text?

_____

_____

_____

_____

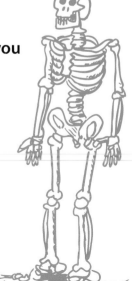

# Comprehension Review

**Fill in the best answer for each question.**

**❶ What can you conclude about the cardiac muscle?**
Ⓐ It is not necessary for the body.
Ⓑ It is exactly like skeletal muscle.
Ⓒ It does not tire quickly.
Ⓓ It is attached to bones.

**❷ Which of these would probably happen *without* a skeletal system?**
Ⓐ It would be easier to catch diseases.
Ⓑ The heart would not have cardiac muscle.
Ⓒ Smooth muscles would not help in swallowing.
Ⓓ The brain would be very well protected.

**❸ Skeletal muscles probably _____**
Ⓐ keep your heart beating.
Ⓑ work on their own.
Ⓒ are attached to bones.
Ⓓ come in pairs.

**❹ The author compares the body to _____**
Ⓐ the cardiac muscle.
Ⓑ a machine.
Ⓒ a gene.
Ⓓ a joint.

**❺ What is one effect of muscles coming in pairs?**
Ⓐ This is the framework for the body.
Ⓑ Your body's systems work together.
Ⓒ Bones are held together.
Ⓓ This allows you to move.

**❻ The _____ is the framework for the body.**
Ⓐ vital organ
Ⓑ cardiac muscle
Ⓒ muscular system
Ⓓ skeletal system

# Word Power

**Choose the English word from the Vocabulary list that correctly matches the definition.**

 a part of the cell that controls what living things look like, how they grow and behave, etc.

 2 a characteristic that makes one person different from another

 to control or influence something directly, or to decide what will happen

 4 to receive by genetic transmission; to come into possession of

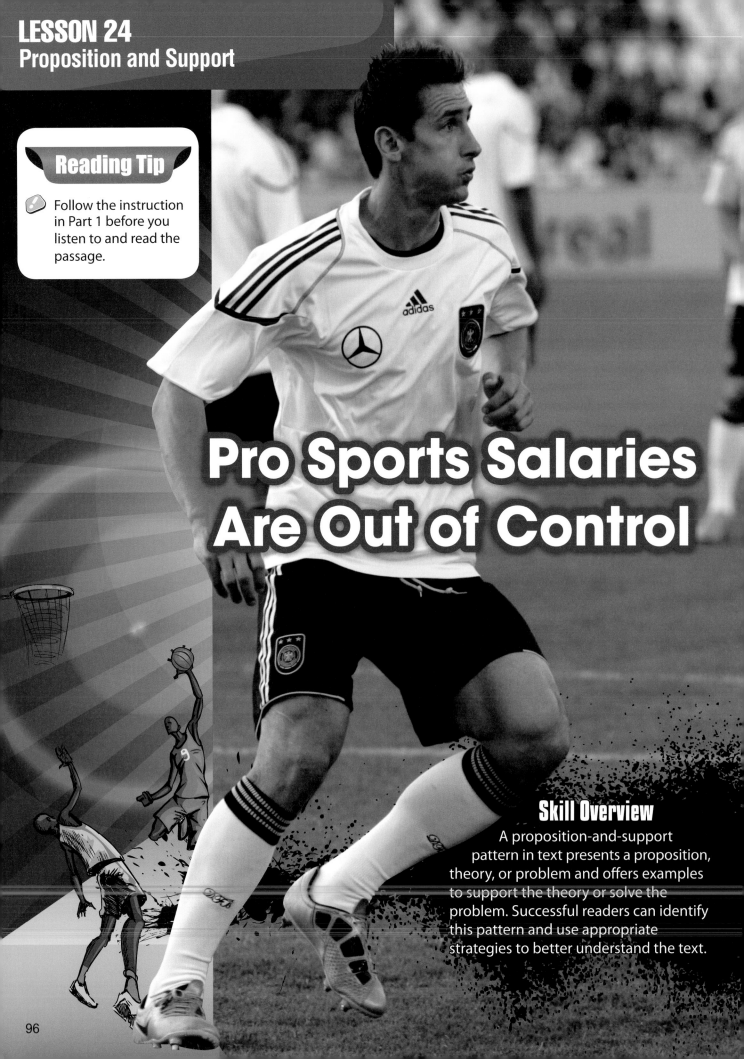

**Reading Tip**

Follow the instruction in Part 1 before you listen to and read the passage.

# Pro Sports Salaries Are Out of Control

## Skill Overview

A proposition-and-support pattern in text presents a proposition, theory, or problem and offers examples to support the theory or solve the problem. Successful readers can identify this pattern and use appropriate strategies to better understand the text.

Which job do you think is more important—leading the country or hitting a baseball? Most people would choose the first job; however, many baseball players and other **professional athletes** make several times the amount of money that the president of a country earns each year. It's time to **limit** the **salaries** of pro athletes.

Some athletes get paid millions of dollars a year. In return, they attend training camps for several weeks a year and play a team sport for a few months. For baseball and basketball players, this means playing several games a week. Football players play one game a week. So these athletes are getting paid for working fewer hours than the average person. At the same time, doctors and teachers work at least 40 hours a week for a tiny percentage of an athlete's salary.

Huge salaries for pro athletes have hurt sports fans. To pay these salaries, teams have raised ticket prices. Thus, many sports fans cannot **afford** to see their favorite teams in person. Also, some teams have only hurt themselves by paying multimillion-dollar salaries to athletes. After paying one athlete an **enormous** amount of money, a team may not have enough money to pay other good players. Once again, fans suffer.

Paying huge salaries to athletes sends the wrong message. It says that being a baseball or football player is a greater **feat** than being a teacher, nurse, or judge. Sports **leagues** should help the public see what's really important. They should limit the money paid to professional athletes.

## Vocabulary

**professional**
related to work that needs special training or education

**athlete**
a person who is very good at sports or physical exercise

**limit**
to control something so that it is not greater than a specified amount, number, or level

**salary**
money paid regularly for doing a job

**afford**
to be able to buy or do something because you have enough money or time

**enormous**
huge; very large

✪**feat**
a remarkable achievement

**league**
a group of teams that play a sport in competition with each other

# Reading Skills Comprehension Practice

 **Part 1** Write a supporting statement for each proposition.

| Proposition | Support |
|---|---|
| **Ⓐ** Teachers and other adults on campus must help students who are being bullied at school. | **1.** Bullying can have serious physical and emotional consequences for the victim. <br> **2.** _____ _____ |
| **Ⓑ** Recycling is an easy way for all of us to do our part to help keep Earth clean. | **1.** Recycling materials helps cut down on the waste that ends up in landfills. <br> **2.** _____ _____ |

 **Part 2** Write the proposition from this passage.

_____

_____

 **Part 3** Write three supporting statements for the proposition from Part 2.

**Supporting statement 1** _____

**Supporting statement 2** _____

**Supporting statement 3** _____

# Comprehension Review

**Fill in the best answer for each question.**

____ **①** *It's time to limit the salaries of pro athletes.* **Which sentence *best* supports this proposition?**

Ⓐ Baseball and basketball players play several games a week.

Ⓑ Huge salaries for pro athletes have hurt sports fans.

Ⓒ Once again, fans suffer.

Ⓓ Teams have raised ticket prices.

____ **②** *Thus, many sports fans cannot afford to see their favorite teams in person.* **Which proposition does this support?**

Ⓐ Huge salaries for pro athletes have hurt sports fans.

Ⓑ Paying huge salaries to athletes sends the wrong message.

Ⓒ Some athletes get paid many millions of dollars a year.

Ⓓ Once again, fans suffer.

____ **③** **Which is the *most* important proposition in this passage?**

Ⓐ Once again, fans suffer.

Ⓑ Paying huge salaries to athletes sends the wrong message.

Ⓒ It's time to limit the salaries of pro athletes.

Ⓓ Football players play one game a week.

____ **④** **The author would probably agree that _____**

Ⓐ teachers make too much money.

Ⓑ football players spend too many hours working.

Ⓒ teams are better off when they pay high salaries to players.

Ⓓ athletes make too much money.

____ **⑤** **Why did the author write this?**

Ⓐ to persuade sports leagues to limit athletes' salaries

Ⓑ to warn sports leagues about player safety

Ⓒ to explain the rules of football

Ⓓ to persuade sports leagues to raise baseball players' salaries

____ **⑥** **How do high salaries for athletes hurt sports fans?**

Ⓐ Some athletes are getting paid millions of dollars a week.

Ⓑ Football players play only one game a week.

Ⓒ Teams have raised ticket prices, so sports fans cannot afford to see their favorite teams.

Ⓓ Too many games are played, so fans cannot decide which game to attend.

# Word Power

**Choose the English word from the Vocabulary list that correctly matches the definition.**

 a remarkable achievement

_____

 money paid regularly for doing a job

_____

 huge; very large

_____

 a person who is very good at sports or physical exercise

_____

## Reading Tip

Follow the instruction in Part 1 before you listen to and read the passage.

Graphic features, such as the figures shown on this page, are included in texts to help you better understand the information and to present it in different ways.

## Skill Overview

**Graphic features** include visuals—such as illustrations, photos, diagrams, maps, tables, graphs, and charts—that add meaning to a text. These features help readers get more information from the written page and can convey the information in a clearer or more interesting way.

# THE PYTHAGOREAN THEOREM

Pythagoras was born around 584 B.C. on the Greek island of Samos. He became one of the greatest thinkers of his time. Pythagoras traveled a great deal through many countries. He learned a lot from these travels.

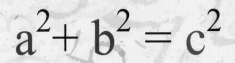

$$a^2 + b^2 = c^2$$

To Pythagoras, mathematics was the most important subject. He believed that "all things are numbers." He looked for mathematical relationships everywhere.

His most **influential** theory was the Pythagorean theorem. This theorem is used to find the length of a side of a right triangle given the length of the other two sides. It is stated this way: In a right triangle, the square of the **hypotenuse** equals the sum of the squares of the other two sides. The hypotenuse is the side of the triangle **opposite** the right angle.

Pythagoras had learned the "3-4-5 triangle" from the Egyptians, who had the mathematical understanding of right angles long before the Greeks did. The Egyptians used a long piece of rope with 12 knots tied an **equal** distance apart. Then they used the rope and stakes to form a right triangle. There would be three knots on one side, four knots on another side, and five knots on the longest side. They used this type of triangle and its **calculations** to **measure** land and create such wonders as the pyramids.

Yet the Egyptians were able to use only geometry in a "hands-on" way. Pythagoras and other Greeks took the development of geometry a step further. After they were able to represent a problem **visually**, they could then understand how to measure and calculate it in their minds. For example, Pythagoras first studied a right triangle by drawing it as the sides of three squares. He was then able to generalize the rule to all right triangles and create the mathematical **formula** $a^2 + b^2 = c^2$. This is the Pythagorean theorem.

Pythagoras was a great thinker. Even today, mathematicians use the theorem that is named for him, as well as many of his other ideas.

## Vocabulary

**influential**
having the ability to affect what others do or think

✪**hypotenuse**
the side of a right triangle opposite the right angle

**opposite**
located across from something

**equal**
the same in amount, number, or size

**calculation**
use of a mathematical process (e.g., addition, subtraction, multiplication, division) to find a number or answer

**measure**
to discover the exact size or amount of something

✪**visually**
relating to seeing or appearance

**formula**
numbers or letters that represent a mathematical rule

**Part 1** Choose a graphic feature from the passage and tell what you learned from it.

_____

_____

_____

_____

_____

_____

$$a^2 + b^2 = c^2$$

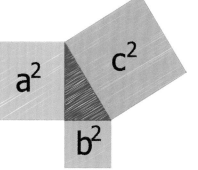

**Part 2** Tell how the graphic features in the passage support the main idea.

_____

_____

_____

_____

**Part 3** Use the graphic feature of the Pythagorean theorem to answer the questions.

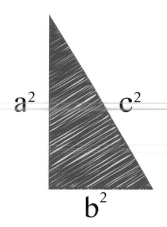

**1.** What do the letters **a**, **b**, and **c** represent?

_____

**2.** What is the mathematical formula for the Pythagorean theorem?

_____

**3.** Which square in the graphic is the largest? Why?

_____

# Comprehension Review

**Fill in the best answer for each question.**

_____ ❶ **What did Pythagoras use to teach his students about the Pythagorean theorem?**
- Ⓐ a prism
- Ⓑ a sphere
- Ⓒ a cube
- Ⓓ a pyramid

_____ ❷ **According to the diagram, which has the _largest_ value?**
- Ⓐ c
- Ⓑ a
- Ⓒ b
- Ⓓ The sides are all equal.

_____ ❸ **What kind of triangle is the subject of the Pythagorean theorem?**
- Ⓐ an equilateral triangle
- Ⓑ a right triangle
- Ⓒ an acute triangle
- Ⓓ an obtuse triangle

_____ ❹ **How was the right triangle useful for the Egyptians?**
- Ⓐ They used it to understand basic structures.
- Ⓑ They used it to calculate math problems.
- Ⓒ They used it to measure land and build pyramids.
- Ⓓ They used it to build houses.

_____ ❺ **Which statement is true?**
- Ⓐ Pythagoras was the first to study right angles.
- Ⓑ Pythagoras believed that "all things are numbers."
- Ⓒ Pythagoras first studied a right triangle by visualizing it.
- Ⓓ Pythagoras learned the 3-4-5 triangle from the Greeks.

_____ ❻ **Unlike the Egyptians, Pythagoras _____**
- Ⓐ used the right triangle to measure land.
- Ⓑ used circles and squares to help him understand triangles.
- Ⓒ studied calculus.
- Ⓓ could calculate mathematical problems in his mind.

# Word Power

**Choose the English word from the Vocabulary list that correctly matches the definition.**

 numbers or letters that represent a mathematical rule

_____

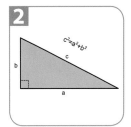 the side of a right triangle opposite the right angle

_____

 having the ability to affect what others do or think

_____

 use of a mathematical process (e.g., addition, subtraction, multiplication, division) to find a number or answer

_____

A hibernating dormouse

## Reading Tip

- Follow the instruction in Part 1 before you listen to and read the passage.

- While listening to and reading the passage, underline information that is confusing to you.

- You should also try to adjust your reading speed for different kinds of texts.

# HIBERNATION

## Skill Overview

Readers who can self-monitor understand when they are confused by a section of text, when a text does not make sense, and when they are reading too quickly or too slowly. They are then able to modify their own reading habits to ensure that they understand the text.

26

**Hibernation** is a seasonal **adaptation** by animals that live in cold climates. Many animals hibernate, including marsupials, insectivores, fruit bats, primates, and carnivores. These animals hibernate to escape the stresses of food **shortage** and unpleasant winter weather. During hibernation, the **metabolic rate** of the animal's body goes down. This means the body reduces the amount of energy it needs. Needing less energy, the sleeping animal can survive on its **reserve** of stored fat.

## Vocabulary

**hibernation**
the act of sleeping through the winter

**adaptation**
an adjustment to one's environment or surroundings

**shortage**
a situation in which there is not enough of something

⊘**metabolic rate**
a measure of a body's energy needs

**reserve**
a supply of something that is stored for later use

**sensitive**
easily influenced, changed, or damaged, especially by a physical activity or effect

**disturb**
to interrupt what someone is doing

**active**
doing things that require moving and using energy

Even in hibernation, however, the animal can sense danger. Certain parts of the brain are **sensitive** to changes in noise, light, odor, and severe cold. Hibernating animals that sense these events will wake up quickly.

Animals need energy to enter hibernation. They also need energy to come out of it. So it would seem natural that they would stay in hibernation all the way until spring. However, they do not. Even if they are not **disturbed**, hibernating animals wake up every so often. For example, bears give birth during hibernation. Even mammals that sleep more deeply than bears will wake up during certain periods.

During periodic awakenings, an animal cycles through four stages. First, the animal is normally **active**. Then, its body temperature drops over a period of 12 to 24 hours. Next, the animal sleeps from hours to weeks, depending on the species. Last, the animal wakes up, and its body temperature starts to rise again. A hibernating mammal may cycle through these phases many times during the winter season. For example, during observations of several hibernating American badgers in Wyoming, one badger went through the cycle 30 times. This was during just one period of hibernation. But even when awake, the badgers in the study stayed underground for 70 days in a row. Because they did, the badgers used much less energy than they would have if they had been active in the cold air aboveground.

# Reading Skills Comprehension Practice

 **Part 1**   Think about strategies you have used to monitor your reading. Record them in the web below.

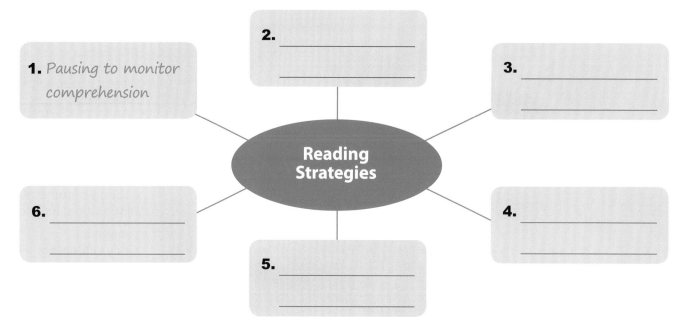

**1.** Pausing to monitor comprehension

**2.** _____ _____

**3.** _____ _____

**Reading Strategies**

**6.** _____ _____

**5.** _____ _____

**4.** _____ _____

 **Part 2**   Answer the questions below.

**1.** What have you done when you became confused while reading?

_____

**2.** Did your confusion prevent you from completely understanding the text?

_____

**3.** List three things you can do if you become confused while reading a text.

_____

**Part 3**   List the reading strategies you used to help you understand this text.

_____

_____

_____

# Comprehension Review

**Fill in the best answer for each question.**

_____ **❶** *During periodic awakenings, an animal cycles through four stages.*

**If you did not know what *periodic* means, what could you do?**

Ⓐ reread the title
Ⓑ write the word
Ⓒ read more of the passage
Ⓓ read the word aloud

_____ **❷ What should you read if you forgot the topic of this passage?**

Ⓐ a dictionary
Ⓑ the title and caption
Ⓒ the index
Ⓓ the last sentence

_____ **❸ If you forgot what kind of animals hibernate, what could you do?**

Ⓐ look at a map
Ⓑ read the title and headings
Ⓒ look up the words in a dictionary
Ⓓ read the passage again

_____ **❹ Which is *not* a reason why animals hibernate?**

Ⓐ to escape from predators
Ⓑ to escape the stresses of food shortage
Ⓒ to take cover during unpleasant winter weather
Ⓓ to conserve energy

_____ **❺ The process of periodic awakening is _____**

Ⓐ a short process.
Ⓑ a two-part cycle.
Ⓒ a four-part cycle.
Ⓓ seasonal.

_____ **❻ According to the passage, which statement about hibernating animals is true?**

Ⓐ Their metabolic rate goes down.
Ⓑ Their body temperature rises.
Ⓒ They only need energy to come out of hibernation.
Ⓓ They remain in hibernation until spring.

# Word Power

**Choose the English word from the Vocabulary list that correctly matches the definition.**

 an adjustment to one's environment or surroundings

_____

 a measure of a body's energy needs

_____

 to interrupt what someone is doing

_____

 the act of sleeping through the winter

_____

# The Book That Caused an Uproar

Uncle Tom and Little Eva from *Uncle Tom's Cabin*

## Reading Tip

Texts often include picture captions that help you understand what you are reading.

## Skill Overview

A **caption** is one or two words or a sentence that **summarizes a photograph or an illustration**. It may be possible to get as much information from picture caption as from the text.

🎧 27

Harriet Beecher was the daughter of a famous **preacher** who spoke publicly **against** slavery. Harriet was one of 11 children. Many of the children followed in their father's footsteps and also spoke out against slavery.

In 1836, Harriet married Calvin Stowe, a **professor** and an author. He wanted his wife to write, too. Harriet wrote many books, but she is best known for *Uncle Tom's Cabin*. This book follows the lives of two slave families and **depicts** the **horrors** of slavery.

At first, the story was printed for 40 weeks in a newspaper. The chapters were read weekly in homes across the country. The entire book was printed in March 1852. *Uncle Tom's Cabin* immediately broke all sales records, selling 50,000 copies by 1857.

This story **ignited** the antislavery cause. It was more **meaningful** than **protests** and preaching. The book had a personal style, interesting characters, and everyday settings. All of this made the book very popular, especially in the North.

**Harriet Beecher Stowe**

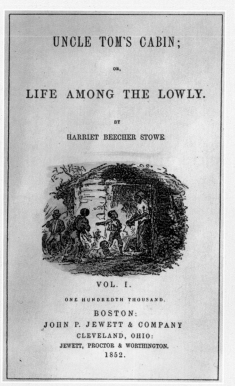

UNCLE TOM'S CABIN;

OR,

LIFE AMONG THE LOWLY.

BY

HARRIET BEECHER STOWE.

VOL. I.

ONE HUNDREDTH THOUSAND.

BOSTON:
JOHN P. JEWETT & COMPANY
CLEVELAND, OHIO:
JEWETT, PROCTOR & WORTHINGTON.
1852.

*Uncle Tom's Cabin* **made many people in the South angry.**
**Some Southerners were so upset that if you were caught with the book, you could be sent to jail.**

# Reading Skills Comprehension Practice

**Part 1** Describe how the pictures and picture captions helped you understand this passage. Then describe how it would have been different without them.

**Part 2** Describe why people in the South were so upset when Uncle Tom's Cabin was published based on the passage and the captions.

**Part 3** Choose a picture from the passage and write a picture caption for it.

VOL. I.

The author of Uncle Tom's Cabin, Harriet Beecher Stowe.

# Comprehension Review

**Fill in the best answer for each question.**

_____ **1** How did Southerners feel about *Uncle Tom's Cabin*?

Ⓐ Most Southerners loved the book.

Ⓑ Many were angry about the book.

Ⓒ *Uncle Tom's Cabin* was more popular in the South than in the North.

Ⓓ They could not understand the book.

_____ **2** What could have happened to Southerners caught with *Uncle Tom's Cabin*?

Ⓐ They could have gotten prizes.

Ⓑ They could have been killed.

Ⓒ They could have gone to jail.

Ⓓ They could have moved to the North.

_____ **3** The caption tells you that _____ was the book that caused an uproar.

Ⓐ *Uncle Tom's Cabin*

Ⓑ *Moby Dick*

Ⓒ Harriet Beecher Stowe

Ⓓ Calvin Stowe

_____ **4** Why was *Uncle Tom's Cabin* so meaningful?

Ⓐ It was popular in the South.

Ⓑ It had a personal style, interesting characters, and everyday settings.

Ⓒ It was about Harriet Beecher Stowe.

Ⓓ It supported slavery.

_____ **5** Harriet Beecher Stowe probably thought that _____

Ⓐ people should not speak out against slavery.

Ⓑ writing about slaves was not a good idea.

Ⓒ the South was right about slavery.

Ⓓ slavery was wrong.

_____ **6** *Uncle Tom's Cabin* was _____

Ⓐ first printed in a newspaper.

Ⓑ extremely unpopular in the North.

Ⓒ about very rich families.

Ⓓ Harriet Beecher Stowe's only book.

# Word Power

**Choose the English word from the Vocabulary list that correctly matches the definition.**

 to set in motion

_____

 to represent or portray

_____

 a strong complaint expressing disagreement, disapproval, or opposition

_____

 a university teacher

_____

# NELSON MANDELA

MAKE POVERTY HISTORY

## Reading Tip

- This passage is a biography about Nelson Mandela.

- **Biographies** are often written in chronological order, starting with the earliest events in a person's life and continuing to the most recent events.

## Skill Overview

Authors structure their writing so that readers can easily understand the information. Text that is written in chronological order tells the time order in which a series of events occurred. Developing an awareness of chronological order helps readers to better understand a text.

🎧 28

South Africa gained its **independence** from Great Britain in 1934. This was very early in the twentieth century compared to when other African nations gained their independence. But in the new, free South Africa, not every South African person was free. South Africa was **governed** by white people. Whites were a minority in the country. The black people outnumbered the whites by a large numbery, yet, they had no voice in how they were governed.

Beginning in 1948, South Africa had an official policy of **apartheid**. Apartheid is related to the English word apart. It means that white and black people must be separated. This **policy** had been in place for many centuries. But in 1948, it became a law. Blacks did not have citizenship. They were forced to live in small areas called *bantustans*, or homelands. Many jobs, parks, beaches, and stores were for whites only. Black and white people could not marry.

Nelson Mandela was a leader of the black majority. Before apartheid became a law, he became the secretary of the African National Congress Youth League (ANCYL). Mandela and the ANCYL organized strikes, **boycotts**, and acts of civil disobedience. He did these things to protest the white government's actions.

In 1960, Mandela's organization was outlawed. Mandela was **arrested** for **treason**, but he was found not guilty. Mandela soon formed a military group to fight against the government. He and others were frustrated. Years of peaceful protests had brought no change for black South Africans. In 1962, he was again arrested for planning to **overthrow** the government of South Africa. He was found guilty and sentenced to life in prison. As a black man, Mandela was not allowed equal treatment in the courts.

Mandela was released from prison in 1990. He continued to work for freedom. He has said that many of his military tactics were wrong. But he has never apologized for working for the black people of South Africa. He was awarded the Nobel Peace Prize in 1993. In 1994, Mandela was elected the first black president of South Africa. This was the first South African election in which blacks were able to vote.

## Vocabulary

**independence**
freedom from being governed or ruled by another country

**govern**
to control and direct the public business of a country, city, group of people, etc.

✪**apartheid**
racial segregation that used to exist in South Africa

**policy**
a set of ideas or a plan of what to do in a particular situation that has been agreed upon officially by a group of people, a business organization, a government, or a political party

**boycott**
an organized refusal to do something or buy something, as a way of protest

**arrest**
to use the power of the law to take and keep someone

**treason**
the crime of acting against a government

**overthrow**
to defeat or remove someone from power, using force

# Reading Skills Comprehension Practice

**Part 1** List some topics or texts that follow a chronological order.

1. *biographies*

2.

3.

4.

**Part 2** Explain why the author chose to write about Nelson Mandela in chronological order.

_____

_____

_____

**Part 3** Record key events from the passage to show that it is written in chronological order.

| Year | Event |
|------|-------|
| 1934 | |
| 1948 | |
| 1960 | |
| 1962 | |
| 1990 | |
| 1993 | |
| 1994 | |

# Comprehension Review

**Fill in the best answer for each question.**

_____ ❶ **Mandela went to prison** *after* _____
- Ⓐ winning the Nobel Peace Prize.
- Ⓑ becoming president of South Africa.
- Ⓒ forming a military group to fight against the government.
- Ⓓ the first South African election in which blacks were able to vote.

_____ ❷ **Which of these happened** *first*?
- Ⓐ Apartheid became law.
- Ⓑ Nelson Mandela became South Africa's first black president.
- Ⓒ Nelson Mandela went to prison.
- Ⓓ Blacks were forced to live in bantusans.

_____ ❸ **The African National Congress Youth League (ANCYL) was outlawed** *before* _____
- Ⓐ blacks had no citizenship.
- Ⓑ blacks were forced to live in bantusans.
- Ⓒ apartheid became law.
- Ⓓ Nelson Mandela was arrested.

_____ ❹ **What is this passage** *mostly* **about?**
- Ⓐ life in a South African prison
- Ⓑ Nelson Mandela's life
- Ⓒ the history of slavery
- Ⓓ people who have won the Nobel Peace Prize

_____ ❺ **Why do you think Mandela's organization was outlawed?**
- Ⓐ His organization believed in apartheid.
- Ⓑ His organization supported the government.
- Ⓒ Mandela was too popular with the people.
- Ⓓ His organization protested the government's actions.

_____ ❻ **Which one of these was** *not* **part of apartheid?**
- Ⓐ Blacks and whites could not marry.
- Ⓑ Blacks were forced to live in bantusans.
- Ⓒ Blacks had full citizenship.
- Ⓓ Many beaches, parks, and stores were for whites only.

# Word Power

**Choose the English word from the Vocabulary list that correctly matches the definition.**

the crime of acting against a government

_____

an organized refusal to do something or buy something, as a way of protest

_____

segregation that used to exist in South Africa

to use the power of the law to take and keep someone

# Henri Matisse

## Skill Overview

**Facts** are **true statements**, whereas **opinions** reflect one's **feelings or emotions**. Readers must distinguish between facts and opinions in order to read a text critically and understand the author's point of view.

### Reading Tip

- This passage is a biography about Henri Matisse, a famous artist.

- It contains many facts about Matisse's life. The author also includes opinions about the topic.

One of the most important artists of the twentieth century was Frenchman Henri Matisse. He led an art movement called *post-Impressionism* and was one of the first famous **collage** artists. Throughout his career, Matisse experimented with different colors, art forms, and **mediums**. He did not follow the established rules of art; he created his own.

When Matisse was a young man, a twist of fate led him to become an artist. While training to become a lawyer, he had to have surgery. During his recovery, his mother bought him paints and a how-to book. From then on, Matisse was totally **devoted** to art. Matisse was encouraged in his artistic pursuits by his talented and creative mother. His father took a dim view of his son's new career path. As Matisse was leaving for Paris, his father yelled out, "You'll starve!" However, his father supported him during hard times in the years that followed.

*Landscape with Brook*

Matisse studied at important art academies. Throughout these early years, he copied the Impressionist style of painting and the Japanese style of woodblock prints. As he came in contact with other styles, his work **gradually** changed.

In 1904, Matisse had his first one-man show, which met with little success. But by the following year, he was the leader of the Fauvist movement, which relied on bright colors and **distorted** shapes. Critics were shocked by the new forms and called them "the work of wild beasts," or *fauvism* in French. The effects of this short movement have been felt in the art world ever since.

Matisse's style of painting brought **harmony** of space and color to his work. His paintings were simple, but **radiant** and bright in color. They were not meant to be realistic, but rather focused on form, not subject. He focused on lines, colors, textures, and arrangement of objects in order to achieve the proper form.

Matisse did more than just paint. He also opened his own art academy for children and published a book about his artistic beliefs. Later, he created murals, stage designs for a ballet, book illustrations, sculptures, and collages. Matisse's collages were some of his most important pieces of work. Amazingly, he created many of them when he was in his eighties and sick in bed. He would instruct his assistants to paint huge pieces of paper with bright colors. Then he would cut out the shapes. As directed, the assistants pinned the shapes onto white paper and then pasted them down.

Matisse was a man with a **mischievous** personality and keen sense of humor—characteristics that are reflected in his artwork. As a master of color, he brought a special joyfulness and a childlike perspective to his art. When Matisse died in 1954, he left a part of himself behind for future generations to enjoy.

## Vocabulary

**collage**
a work of art made from many different materials glued on a surface

**medium**
a particular form or system of communication

**devoted**
to have a strong passion or sense of loyalty to someone or something

**gradually**
happening little by little over time

**distorted**
changed from the usual, original, natural, or intended form

**harmony**
a situation in which things seem right or suitable together

**radiant**
bright and shining

**mischievous**
behaving in a way that is slightly bad but is not intended to cause serious harm or damage

**Woman with a Hat**

**Icarus**

*Polynesia, the sky*

**Portrait of Pierre Matisse**

# Reading Skills Comprehension Practice

**Part 1** Record two facts and two opinions from the passage.

**Fact**

1. Matisse led an art movement called post-Impressionism.
2. _____
3. _____

**Opinion**

1. Matisse was a man with a mischievous personality and keen sense of humor.
2. _____
3. _____

**Part 2** Read the statements below. Write "F" if it is a fact and "O" if it is an opinion.

1. _____ The Metropolitan Museum of Art is located in New York City.

2. _____ The portrait that is hanging on the wall of the studio is the most compelling that I've ever seen.

3. _____ Fall weather is the most enjoyable because of all the changing colors in nature.

4. _____ Fall is one of the four seasons; the other are spring, summer, and winter.

**Part 3** Complete the chart below with facts and opinions about four different topics.

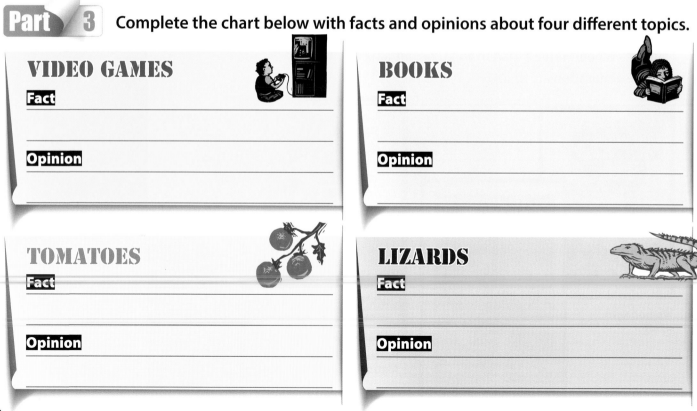

**VIDEO GAMES**

Fact
_____

Opinion
_____

**BOOKS**

Fact
_____

Opinion
_____

**TOMATOES**

Fact
_____

Opinion
_____

**LIZARDS**

Fact
_____

Opinion
_____

# Comprehension Review

**Fill in the best answer for each question.**

**1 Which of these is an opinion?**

Ⓐ Matisse's style of painting brought harmony of space and color to his work.

Ⓑ "You'll starve!"

Ⓒ Throughout his career, Matisse experimented with different colors, art forms, and mediums.

Ⓓ While training to become a lawyer, he had to have surgery.

**2 Which one of these tells you what someone thinks?**

Ⓐ His father later supported him during hard times.

Ⓑ Then he would cut out the shapes.

Ⓒ He copied the Impressionist style of painting.

Ⓓ Critics were shocked by the new forms.

**3 Which statement is a fact?**

Ⓐ The assistants pinned the shapes onto white paper and then pasted them down.

Ⓑ "You'll starve!"

Ⓒ Matisse was a man with a mischievous personality and a keen sense of humor.

Ⓓ He brought a special joyfulness and a childlike perspective to his art.

**4 Some of Matisse's most important works were _____**

Ⓐ murals.

Ⓑ sculptures.

Ⓒ collages.

Ⓓ portraits.

**5 Which statement is false?**

Ⓐ Henri Matisse was a twentieth-century artist.

Ⓑ Fauvism was very popular with art critics.

Ⓒ Matisse started by copying the Impressionist style.

Ⓓ Matisse painted *Woman with a Hat*.

**6 The author wants you to _____**

Ⓐ appreciate the work of Henri Matisse.

Ⓑ visit Matisse's birthplace.

Ⓒ learn to paint.

Ⓓ dislike art.

# Word Power

**Choose the English word from the Vocabulary list that correctly matches the definition.**

**1**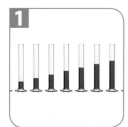
happening little by little over time

_____

**2**
a work of art made from many different materials glued on a surface

_____

**3**
to have a strong passion or sense of loyalty to someone or something

_____

**4**
changed from the usual, original, natural, or intended form

_____

# Birth of an Island

## Reading Tip

- Follow the instruction in Part 1 before you listen to and read the passage.

- Asking questions helps you clarify or elaborate on ideas.

## Skill Overview

Good readers ask questions before, during, and after reading. When readers are thinking of questions as they read, they are monitoring their own comprehension and reading for a particular purpose.

🎧 30

    Islands aren't born very often. Sometimes islands are created when a **volcano erupts** below the surface of the ocean. The **lava** cools and builds the volcano up until it **eventually** gets tall enough to poke through the surface of the ocean.

In 1963, a crew on a fishing boat was present when one island was being born. Early one morning, the boat was sailing near the coast of Iceland, and the crew smelled something suspicious; however, no one knew what the source of the smell was. Suddenly, the boat began rocking back and forth. The calm sea now began to rage, spitting out billows of dark, ominous smoke. The terrified crew stood in awe as they watched an **underground** volcano erupting right in front of their eyes!

The captain and his crew moved the vessel and watched from a distance as the volcano **spit** rock and lava into the air. It looked like the sky was raining rocks. The volcano erupted for days until the fires finally burned themselves out. The top of the volcano was sticking out of the ocean. When the lava on top of the volcano cooled, a new island sat where only water had been before.

Scientists were very excited because they had never seen a brand-new island. The scientists named the new island *Surtsey*, after the Icelandic god of fire.

But the new island did not **resemble** other islands—it was only a pile of bare rocks. There were no plants or animals on it. Scientists wondered how life would come to an empty island. They watched and waited for many months, and eventually a single plant began growing on the rocks. Scientists found that birds would often land on the island and drop plant material or seeds that had been trapped in their feathers and claws.

Today, there are a number of birds and plants living on Surtsey. Except for a few scientists, however, humans are not allowed to visit the island. It is the perfect place to learn about how plants and animals **inhabit** new places.

## Vocabulary

**volcano**
a mountain with a large, circular hole at the top through which lava gases, steam, and dust are being or have been forced out

**erupt**
to send out rocks, ash, lava, etc., in a sudden explosion

**lava**
hot liquid rock

**eventually**
after a while

**underground**
below the surface of Earth

**spit**
to push or throw out something, especially while burning

**resemble**
to look like something or someone

**inhabit**
to live in a place

**The island of Surtsey**

# Reading Skills Comprehension Practice

**Part 1** List the questions that you have about this passage, based on the title and the topic.

1. How can an island be born?

2. _____

3. _____

**Part 2** List the questions you have that will help **clarify** information in the passage.

1. Can scientists predict the development of an island?

2. _____

3. _____

**Part 3** List the questions you have that **elaborate** on something you read in the passage.

1. How far away did the fishing boat have to move to get out of danger?

2. _____
   _____

3. _____
   _____

4. _____
   _____

5. _____
   _____

# Comprehension Review

**Fill in the best answer for each question.**

_____ **1** *Sometimes islands are created when a volcano erupts below the surface of the ocean.*

**Which question does this sentence answer?**

Ⓐ How many volcanoes are there?

Ⓑ How are islands created?

Ⓒ Where is the island of Surtsey?

Ⓓ How did Surtsey get its name?

_____ **2** **What did Surtsey look like at first?**

**Which statement answers this question?**

Ⓐ The lava cools and builds the volcano up.

Ⓑ Finally, after many months, a single plant began growing on the rocks.

Ⓒ But no one knew what the source of the smell was.

Ⓓ It was only a pile of bare rocks.

_____ **3** **Which question is *not* answered in this passage?**

Ⓐ How does a volcano form an island?

Ⓑ How did the island of Surtsey get its name?

Ⓒ How many volcanic islands are there?

Ⓓ What is Surtsey like now?

_____ **4** *...spitting out billows of dark, ominous smoke.*

**What does the word _ominous_ mean?**

Ⓐ very frightening

Ⓑ sweet

Ⓒ musical

Ⓓ joyful

_____ **5** **Why do you think humans are not allowed to visit Surtsey?**

Ⓐ Lava is still flowing from the volcano, so it is still too dangerous for humans.

Ⓑ No plants or animals.

Ⓒ There are no boats or planes that go to Surtsey.

Ⓓ Humans might destroy the life on Surtsey, and scientists want to study how plants and animals spread.

_____ **6** **How did Surtsey change from a pile of bare rocks to an island with plants and animals?**

Ⓐ Scientists planted trees on the island and moved animals there.

Ⓑ Birds landed on the island and dropped seeds and material from their feathers and claws.

Ⓒ People built bridges.

Ⓓ People visiting Surtsey brought seeds and plants with them.

# Word Power

**Choose the English word from the Vocabulary list that correctly matches the definition.**

 after a while

_____

 to live in a place

_____

 to look like something or someone

_____

 to send out rocks, ash, lava, etc., in a sudden explosion

_____

# Review Test

**Questions 1–10:** Read the passage and look at the diagram. Then answer the questions on the following pages. Fill in the answer choice you think is correct.

## OUR SUN

The Sun is the nearest star to Earth. Not only is the Sun the center of the solar system, it is also central to our lives. This huge ball of gas is so big, more than a million Earths could fit inside it. The Sun holds about 99 percent of all the mass of the solar system. The Sun is a medium-sized yellow star and is incredibly hot, giving off huge amounts of energy. It does this by changing five million tons of matter into energy each second. This energy comes from the Sun's core, where the temperature is about 27,000,000°F (15,000,000°C). The process that produces this incredible heat and energy is called *nuclear fusion.* At the core, the Sun's enormous gravity makes hydrogen atoms fuse into helium atoms. When this happens, a great amount of energy is produced.

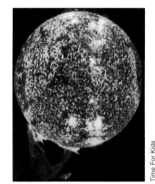

This photo of the Sun, taken with a special filter, shows a huge solar flare.

The energy, in the form of radiation, travels from the core to the Sun's surface. From the surface, it travels outward into our solar system. It takes 8.13 minutes for the energy to reach our planet. But it's worth the wait: the Sun's energy provides us with light and heat. Without this energy, no life could exist on Earth.

**PHOTOSPHERE**
The surface of the Sun that we see.

**CONVECTIVE ZONE**
The energy from below is carried to the surface by currents of gas that rise (and eventually fall back).

**RADIATIVE ZONE**
Energy moves out of the core and through this area.

**CORE**
The center of the Sun, where nuclear fusion takes place. More than half the Sun's mass is located in this region, even though it takes up only 2 percent of its volume.

**CHROMOSPHERE**

**CORONA**

**Sunspots**

**Prominence**

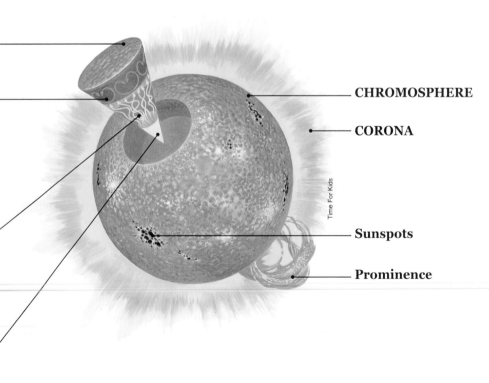

## The Surface and Above

The Sun's surface is called the *photosphere*. This word is Greek for "sphere of light." The photosphere looks like a solid yellow surface, but it is really a swirling ocean of blazing gases 300 miles thick. The temperature here is about 10,000°F (5,500°C).

Above its surface are the gases that form the Sun's atmosphere. The middle region of these gases is called the *chromosphere*. Above the chromosphere is the *corona*, which is visible around the Sun during a solar eclipse.

## Photosphere Activity

**Sunspots:** Dark spots often appear on the surface of the Sun. These Sunspots range in size from less than 600 miles across to about 60,000 miles across. They sometimes last weeks before disappearing. What makes these dark blotches? Scientists believe they are cool spots, caused by magnetic fields holding gases from reaching the surface. They aren't really black, just a little darker than the surrounding area.

**Prominences:** Giant clouds of gas often rise above the Sun's atmosphere. They look like loops, which arch down onto the surface or sometimes flare out into space.

**Flares:** Solar flares are bursts of hot gases that shoot deep into the solar system. When they reach Earth, they can disrupt radio communications.

---

**1** Why might a person read this article?

Lesson 1

- (A) to read about the planets
- (B) to find out about how the Sun's rays travel
- (C) to find out about space travel
- (D) to get information about the Sun

**2** The pictures, headings, and title tell you that you will learn about _____

Lesson 2

- (A) the planets.
- (B) the Sun.
- (C) how to save energy.
- (D) how Earth orbits the Sun.

**3** What is the main idea of the first paragraph?

Lesson 5

- (A) The Sun is the nearest star to Earth.
- (B) Nuclear fusion produces incredible heat and energy.
- (C) The Sun holds about 99 percent of all the mass of the solar system.
- (D) The Sun is our nearest star; it is both very large and very hot.

**4** The title is a good clue that you will not read about _____

Lesson 6

- (A) the parts of the Sun.
- (B) how the Sun makes energy.
- (C) how the moon orbits Earth.
- (D) why the Sun is important.

**5** People who want to learn about _____ would probably read this.

Lesson 7

- (A) science
- (B) cooking
- (C) math
- (D) the oceans

**6** *"The Surface and Above"*
The heading tells you that this section is **mostly** about _____

Lesson 10

- (A) Earth's orbit.
- (B) the inner part of the Sun.
- (C) what the surface of the Sun is like.
- (D) how the Sun makes energy.

**7** *The Sun's surface is called the photosphere.*

Which piece of information will probably be in this paragraph?                    Lesson 11

- Ⓐ the size of the Sun
- Ⓑ the color of the Sun's surface
- Ⓒ Earth's distance from the Sun
- Ⓓ the temperature of the Sun's core

**8** When solar flares reach Earth, they can cause _____                    Lesson 13

- Ⓐ the corona.
- Ⓑ bursts of hot gases.
- Ⓒ disruption in radio communications.
- Ⓓ temperature changes.

**9** Why do you think the Sun is a ball of gases and not a solid?                    Lesson 16

- Ⓐ Dark spots often appear on the surface of the Sun.
- Ⓑ The Sun is too small to be solid.
- Ⓒ The Sun is at the center of our solar system.
- Ⓓ The Sun is too hot for gases to change to solids.

**10** One important difference between Earth and the Sun is that _____                    Lesson 18

- Ⓐ Earth is not in the solar system, but the Sun is.
- Ⓑ the Sun is not in the solar system, but Earth is.
- Ⓒ the Sun is a ball of gases, but Earth is not.
- Ⓓ Earth has a surface, but the Sun does not.

**Questions 11–20:** Read the passage and then answer the questions on the following page. Fill in the answer choice you think is correct.

# A Family That Digs Together...

Adrian, Elyse, and Aubrey sift through soil taken from a tomb.

Photos: Courtesy Diane Z. Chase/Caraçol Archaeological Project

## The Chases have made exciting discoveries in the ancient Mayan city of Caraçol

By Kathryin Hoffman

Crawling around creepy tombs is not a typical pastime for a 9-year-old boy, but it's routine for Aubrey Chase, his brother Adrian, 11, and their sister Elyse, 6. Their parents, Arlen and Diane, are archaeologists—scientists who study the remains of old civilizations. Both teach at the University of Central Florida. They spend two months a year exploring the ruins of an ancient city called Caraçol (Car-ah-COAL) in Belize, Central America.

Even though it is very hot, Adrian must wear long sleeves and pants to guard against sunburn and insects.

This is the view in Caraçol from above the Mayan palace called Caana, which is Mayan for "sky palace."

The Mayas, native people of Central America and Mexico, built Caraçol more than 2,000 years ago. It is one of the largest Mayan cities ever found. Arlen and Diane Chase have been studying Caraçol's ancient temples and tombs for 17 years, searching for clues about the Mayas and how they lived.

## Treasures in the Dirt

While in Belize, the Chases live in a hut without running water and sleep in hammocks. The kids work with their parents at the dig site every day after morning lessons. The three have found pieces of stone tools and clay pots. "They're really good at fitting the pieces together," says the mom. "It's like a jigsaw puzzle, but not so neat." The kids take part in almost all the excavation activities, including sifting dirt through screens and washing the pieces they find.

Next year, Adrian will begin to make detailed drawings of the excavation.

The Chases have made many fascinating discoveries at Caraçol. This year, they found two new tombs, as well as a very worn-down monument. They realized that they had walked by the monument many times before—it looked like a large stone.

## A Family Adventure

Each of the Chase children has been going to Caraçol since the age of two months! Workers there say the three know a lot about the site. "It's just part of their lives," Diane says. But the experience hasn't grown old. The siblings are surrounded by treasures—in the jungle around Caraçol as well as at the dig site. They have seen many exotic creatures, including toucans, parrots, howler monkeys—and bugs, of course. "There are lots of butterflies, and there are snakes and tarantulas," Elyse told her classmates in an email.

**11** The typeface tells you that this passage has important information about _____
Lesson 15

(A) the Mayas.

(B) the University of Central Florida.

(C) howler monkeys.

(D) the Navajo Indians.

**12** The Chase children probably _____
Lesson 4

(A) have never heard of the Mayas.

(B) don't know much about their parents' work.

(C) don't like to travel.

(D) spend a lot of time outdoors.

**13** Which sentence is another way to tell the information in the first paragraph? Lesson 14

(A) Arlen and Diane Chase are both archaeologists.

(B) The entire Chase family spends two months each year exploring ruins in Belize.

(C) Aubrey Chase is 9 years old.

(D) While in Belize, the Chases live in huts without running water and sleep in hammocks.

**14** What new information about the Mayas does this passage provide? Lesson 19

(A) One of the largest Mayan cities was Caraçol, in Belize.

(B) The Mayas were an ancient people.

(C) The Mayas lived in Central and South America.

(D) The Chase family is from the United States.

**15** *The Chases have made many fascinating discoveries at Caraçol.*

This topic sentence tells you that the paragraph is **mostly** about _____
Lesson 20

(A) the location of Belize.

(B) the history of the Mayan people.

(C) the things that the Chase family has found.

(D) the climate of Caraçol.

**16** *Archaeologists consider the Mayas an advanced civilization.*

Which of these sentences supports this statement? Lesson 24

(A) It is one of the largest Mayan cities ever found.

(B) Scientists say the Mayas had the most advanced writing system of all the native American groups.

(C) Each of the Chase children has been going to Caraçol since the age of two months!

(D) Both teach at the University of Central Florida.

**17** *The picture tells you that Caraçol is located* _____

Lesson 25

- (A) in the jungle.
- (B) next to the ocean.
- (C) in a desert.
- (D) in a very cold climate.

**18** *The kids take part in almost all the excavation activities.*

If you didn't know what happens during an **excavation**, you could _____

Lesson 26

- (A) read the first paragraph again.
- (B) read the title.
- (C) read the rest of the sentence.
- (D) write and say the word.

**19** What do the captions tell you about the climate at Caraçol?

Lesson 27

- (A) It is very windy.
- (B) It is very hot.
- (C) It is too cold for most people to live there.
- (D) It is temperate—not too cold and not too hot.

**20** Which sentence shows an opinion? Lesson 29

- (A) Workers there say the three know a lot about the site.
- (B) It is one of the largest Mayan cities ever found.
- (C) The three have found pieces of stone and clay pots.
- (D) Both teach at the University of Central Florida.

**Questions 21–30:** Read the passage and then answer the questions on the following page. Fill in the answer choice you think is correct.

# Swimming with Sharks

Clark didn't want to admit it, but he was feeling terrified. Everyone else on the boat was smiling and joking; they seemed eager to get in the water on their daylong diving adventure.

"It's not like someone forced you to be here on this ridiculous vacation," Clark said to himself as he gripped the rail so tightly that his knuckles turned white.

As the captain steered farther out to sea, the boat bobbed in the water like a bath toy. "Hey, I can't believe you talked me into this!" Joe said, thrilled that Clark had convinced him to go on this excursion. "Diving with sharks—what an awesome story this will be!"

"Yeah, it'll make a great story," Clark replied. Then he added to himself, "If we live to tell it."

The boat came to a sudden stop, and the captain readied the steel shark cage. The dive instructor delivered instructions, but Clark could barely pay attention; even though he had diving experience, he felt like his heart was in his throat.

When Clark thought no one was looking, he gripped the bars of the shark cage and tugged with the strength of a bull. "They seem strong enough—but exactly how strong do they have to be?" he thought anxiously as he imagined meeting a shark face to face.

"Okay, who's going first?" the dive leader asked.

Before he knew what he was doing, Clark had shot his hand into the air with the speed of a lightning bolt.

Joe assisted Clark with the tanks and handed him the underwater camera. As he stood at the edge of the boat, he looked down into the cage and felt a rush of panic. Soon, he was in the cage and the hatch closed above him with an ominous clamor. His fear quickly disappeared, and all of the familiar habits of years of diving took over.

The cage sunk into the water beneath the boat, slowly descending like a penny sinking to the bottom of a jar. He floated, not frightened, but excited. He remembered now why he had embarked on this journey in the first place.

"What if there aren't any sharks?" he wondered as he peered into the transparent blue water. Just then, a dark, oblong shape appeared just at the edge of his vision, so he lifted the camera into perfect position to prepare for the moment; he had to make sure this was the real thing. As the object came closer and closer, he was certain that it was the formidable creature he had been waiting for. His final thought, as the shark drew near, was that this was going to be an amazing adventure after all!

**21** In this story, Clark's conflict is with _____.  *Lesson 3*

(A) Joe.
(B) the captain.
(C) a shark.
(D) his own fear.

**22** Which word might you use to describe Clark?  *Lesson 8*

(A) bored
(B) adventurous
(C) shy
(D) untrustworthy

**23** Joe helped Clark with the tanks and underwater camera **after** _____  *Lesson 9*

(A) a dark, oblong shape appeared at the edge of Clark's vision.
(B) the cage sank into the water.
(C) Clark shot his hand into the air.
(D) Clark thought that this was going to be an amazing adventure after all.

**24** ...*slowly descending like a penny sinking to the bottom of a jar.*

What is this an example of?  *Lesson 12*

(A) alliteration
(B) personification
(C) a metaphor
(D) a simile

**25** ... *as he gripped the rail so tightly that his knuckles turned white.*

The author describes Clark's knuckles as white to show you that _____  *Lesson 17*

(A) Clark is nervous.
(B) the weather is hot.
(C) Clark and Joe are friends.
(D) the boat is large.

**26** The author uses _____ to show how dangerous the dive could be.  *Lesson 21*

(A) personification
(B) descriptive words such as "ominous"
(C) similes
(D) alliteration

**27** What changes Clark's point of view about the dive?  *Lesson 22*

(A) Clark sees a shark.
(B) A sudden storm comes up.
(C) Joe dives with Clark.
(D) The familiar habits of diving take over.

**28** Which conclusion can you draw from this story?  *Lesson 23*

(A) Sharks are not dangerous.
(B) Joe and Clark do not get along.
(C) Clark enjoys a good adventure.
(D) The boat is not safe.

**29** Which of these happened **last**?  *Lesson 28*

(A) Clark saw a shark.
(B) Joe helped Clark with his tanks.
(C) Clark got into the shark cage.
(D) Clark's fear left him.

**30** Which question is **not** answered in the story?  *Lesson 30*

(A) Who went on the vacation with Clark?
(B) Where did Clark go on his vacation?
(C) Why was Clark nervous at first?
(D) Did Joe dive, too?